"You Americans make me sick," Pulver sneered

The South African cop suddenly kicked the prone Calvin James in the stomach. The black Phoenix Force warrior convulsed in pain and raised his knees to protect his groin and abdomen.

Pulver spat on James. "You think some goddamn. nigger could be a real cop, eh?" Pulver shouted. "No wonder cities in America are jungles of crime and drug abuse, when they don't control black apes like you."

Pulver kicked James again, his boot striking hard against a thigh muscle. "You think you can come to South Africa and kill policemen as if you were still in New York or Chicago?" Pulver snarled. "The hell you will, you stinking savage!"

Mack Bolan's

PHOENIX FORCE

PHOENIX FORCE

Time Bomb

Gar Wilson

A GOLD EAGLE BOOK FROM
WORLDWIDE

TORONTO · NEW YORK · LONDON · PARIS
AMSTERDAM · STOCKHOLM · HAMBURG
ATHENS · MILAN · TOKYO · SYDNEY

First edition March 1986

ISBN 0-373-61322-9

Special thanks and acknowledgment to William Fieldhouse
for his contribution to this work.

Printed in Canada

Author's Note

This book takes place in South Africa. Although it's a work of fiction, I've attempted to make the story technically accurate as well as entertaining. Some readers may regard this book as being too generous with the South African government. Others may feel I've been too critical. A few may also object to certain statements concerning other African countries such as Zimbabwe, Zaire and Uganda.

While researching I carefully cross-checked information with more than one source for accuracy. These sources ranged from the *World Almanac* to various news magazines. I also received considerable material from the South African consulate. Well aware of propaganda, I regarded political statements from this source with suspicion. Anything I could not confirm through other sources has not been included. However, in fairness to the South African consulate, little of its material was propaganda and a surprising amount was actually critical of apartheid. Much of this information held up when cross-checked with other sources. Please bear in mind that propaganda is often based on fact.

I would like to thank the South African consulate for its cooperation. The information it supplied about geography, locations of points of interest, cities and streets, etc., was extremely useful to me in providing the setting for this book. Finally, special thanks to George and Helen Koffman, who shared their nine years of experience in various African countries.

1

"The time has come for us to throw off the chains of oppression!" Reverend Robert Lincoln declared as he faced the crowd that had gathered around the platform. "The time has come for us to stand up and demand equality! The time has come for us to join hands and stand united for freedom!"

Hundreds of hands eagerly clapped in response, while Lincoln loosened his stiff clerical collar. Sweat was making the cloth soggy as the sun burned fiercely in the South African sky. The reverend gazed at the faces in the crowd. Most were black with a few whites and Asians here and there. Lincoln was disappointed. The crowd was smaller than he'd thought it would be. Worse, he counted only three television cameras in the area.

Shit, Lincoln thought. After all that trouble preparing for the Freedom Tour, Lincoln felt they deserved better coverage. Two cameras were from the same American television network, and the third was from a local Johannesburg station. Where was the BBC? Why had the French and the West Germans failed to send TV crews? Had they lost interest in South Africa? Did they think the Reverend Robert Lincoln was talking just to hear his own voice?

Of course, the reverend had a fine voice, trained for public speaking since childhood. Lincoln's sermons packed a real punch. Some criticized him for lecturing about politics and social injustice while seldom quoting Scripture. However, Lincoln believed a minister should preach about whatever subject the Lord chooses. Naturally, politics and social concerns get more media coverage than Scripture.

Forty-one years old, Robert Lincoln was in his prime and at the top of his career as a religious leader and a political activist. A husky black man, Lincoln was an impressive figure. A gold cross hung from his neck and rested in the center of his broad chest. More gold glittered from the diamond-studded rings on his thick fingers and the Rolex watch on his wrist. This never stopped Lincoln from preaching against materialism or about how the rich should do more for the poor.

"The South African government didn't want us to come here," Lincoln told the crowd. "They think I'm a 'rabble-rousin' nigger' who wants to stir up trouble. That's what they think giving equal rights to black people is—trouble. They don't realize their policy of apartheid is the real trouble. It's racism in its worst form. The world condemns South Africa for apartheid and it supports our efforts for freedom for black people in this country—not five years from now, not tomorrow, but *right now*!"

The crowd applauded and cheered. Reverend Lincoln began clapping his hands and stamping his foot in a pulsating rhythm, and soon the majority of the assembly were caught up in the action. The clapping and stomping formed a steady thunder as Lincoln sang a familiar spiritual.

Unfortunately, many of the congregation did not understand English, and only a handful knew the words to the song. The crowd tried to voice support by singing in Swahili, Bantu and several other tribal tongues. Lincoln gamely continued the spiritual, although the mishmash of languages sounded like Saturday night at the Tower of Babel. He hoped the TV people would turn down the audio and dub in the reporters' comments during the singing portion.

"And now, brothers and sisters," Lincoln began, "it is my great pleasure to introduce a true champion of the oppressed. A man who has always strived for the underdog in the United States and throughout the world. My friend and comrade at arms in the battle against injustice, Senator Thomas Finley.''

The crowd applauded as a heavyset man stepped onto the platform. Finley was a familiar figure in American politics. The product of a wealthy Irish Catholic family, Finley had hopped onto the political bandwagon during the Kennedy administration and now rode high in the ranks of liberal democrats.

He spent more time supporting ''appropriate causes'' than on the senate floor and made plenty of speeches in front of the network cameras. He passionately opposed capital punishment and nuclear power and was outraged by American involvement in Latin America and the ''invasion'' of Grenada. When other liberal celebrities were arrested for protesting apartheid at the South African embassy in Washington, and students organized demonstrations at colleges across the nation, Finley decided it was time to join that cause as well.

Reverend Lincoln smiled at Finley as they shook hands. The senator grinned in return and embraced Lincoln. It was a display of unity and affection by two Americans—one white and one black—both concerned with the policy of apartheid. Lincoln's facial expression did not betray his resentment. He had spent half an hour warming up the assembly like a lead-in act for a Las Vegas star performer. Reluctantly, the reverend surrendered the stage to Senator Finley.

''Thank you for that wonderful welcome,'' Finley told the crowd. ''It was certainly more friendly than the greeting we got from the government when we arrived in Johannesburg this morning. They didn't want us to come here, you know. They didn't want to let us talk to you today.''

Finley pointed an accusing finger at two ''Hippos,'' armored assault vans used by the South African military and police. Several uniformed figures stood near the vehicles.

''That is what the government represents!'' Finley exclaimed. ''Brute force, racism and violent oppression.

That's why Reverend Lincoln and I are here. We're opposed to this government's Nazi tactics, and they're afraid of what we've got to say."

The soldiers and police glared at Finley. Ironically, their main concern that day was to protect Senator Finley and Reverend Lincoln if violence occurred. Three Hippos and two dozen cops formed a semicircle around the square. Another Hippo was stationed behind the platform so the Americans could be rushed to safety in an emergency.

The protection had been provided by the South African government—the same government that had allowed Finley and Lincoln into the country so they could carry out their so-called Freedom Tour. The same government that the two Americans were publicly condemning. Would Moscow allow these cheeky bastards to set up a protest rally in the middle of Red Square? The soldiers and cops wished the two Yanks had stayed in the United States.

"Let me tell you what's happening in the world today," Finley continued. "And you Afrikaner Gestapo had better listen, too. People everywhere are demonstrating against this racist regime that denies equality to blacks and other non-whites in South Africa. Americans will no longer buy your gold or diamonds. Americans will no longer do business with this fascist regime. The United Nations has condemned apartheid, and an international ban on trade with South Africa will follow unless apartheid is brought to an end once and forever!"

The senator prepared to continue, but a disturbance in the back rows of the crowd abruptly terminated his speech. A group of marchers had plunged into the crowd, waving signs in several languages. Finley read one that bore the legend in English: Remember Rhodesia. Another sign had the familiar slogan: Yankee Go Home.

Finley was astonished to see the protesters were all blacks and "coloreds," a term that referred to Orientals and mulattoes in South Africa. The antiapartheid rally snarled curses at the counterdemonstrators. Soon both sides were shouting, shoving and throwing punches. Signs crashed down on heads. Fists slammed into faces, and bodies dropped to be kicked and stomped by enraged combatants.

A shrill whistle announced that the police and soldiers were about to join the fray. Tear-gas canisters were lobbed into the crowd, and columns of dense gray mist sputtered from the grenades as the cops donned riot helmets and charged into the battle, swinging batons at the mob. They clubbed antiapartheid proponents and counterdemonstrators alike, showing no favoritism toward either group.

"My God!" Finley gasped. "What's going on?"

"It's a bloody riot, you idiot," a South African army sergeant snapped as he grabbed Finley's arm. "Get the hell off the platform before somebody splits your empty skull with a rock!"

"Wait a minute," the senator began as he turned to face the noncom. He was surprised to discover the sergeant was a large black man with a small diamond pinned to the side of one nostril.

"Move it, you retard!" the sergeant demanded as he shoved Finley toward the rear of the platform.

The senator stumbled down the plank steps and staggered toward the Hippo van. Two white men in uniform quickly grabbed Finley and hauled him to the rear of the riot vehicle. They ignored his protests and roughly pushed the senator into the Hippo.

Reverend Lincoln was already inside the van, sprawled across the floorboards. A ribbon of blood trickled from his split lip. Lincoln was clearly stunned and frightened as he stared up at Finley. Two white troopers climbed inside the Hippo and pulled the doors shut.

"What is the meaning of this?" Finley demanded, turning to face the soldiers.

One of the troopers stepped forward and suddenly lashed a fist into the senator's face. Finley fell to the floor beside Reverend Lincoln. He gasped in astonishment as he placed a hand to his jaw and gazed up at his assailant.

"Just shut your mouth, fat boy," one of the soldiers hissed. His accent wasn't South African. It sounded more American.

"You can't . . ." Finley began, but he decided to heed the man's warning.

"I can't do what, asshole?" the soldier snorted, drawing a pistol from the holster on his hip.

Finley merely shook his head in reply.

"For God's sake," Lincoln said hoarsely. "Don't you realize we're Americans? You're harassing a United States senator and a religious leader. If you don't put that gun away . . ."

The soldier's foot swung, driving the toe of his boot between Lincoln's splayed legs. The reverend shrieked and clasped both hands to his crotch. He convulsed in agony and uttered an ugly choking gasp. Lincoln rolled on his side as a glob of vomit spewed from his open mouth.

"Since you're a preacher," the man said, chuckling, "you don't need your balls, do you, nigger?"

"Our orders are to deliver these two alive, Goodman," the other soldier declared. His voice contained a guttural accent, probably Afrikaans or German.

"Yeah," Goodman agreed, "but nobody said nothin' about whether these bastards had to be in one piece or not. If they give me any more crap, I'm gonna shoot 'em both through the kneecaps, Gruber."

"I suggest you two listen to Goodman," Gruber said, with a sigh. "He is serious. Understand? *Ja?*"

Finley and Lincoln nodded in reply. They heard an engine growl as the Hippo lurched forward. Both men prayed that somehow the abduction would prove to be some sort of bizarre practical joke or perhaps just a bad dream. Yet they would soon learn that the nightmare had just begun.

2

Hal Brognola followed Captain Collins through the corridors of the Nuremburg Military Hospital. His nostrils twitched from the strong odor of disinfectant. Brognola hated the chemically sterile smell of hospitals. The Fed associated hospitals with disease, injury and death.

Hospitals were places for the sick and the maimed. Wrecked bodies were sewn together like torn upholstery. Flesh was cut open to be probed with scalpels and scissors. Hal Brognola had few pleasant memories associated with hospitals. He had seldom entered one unless a friend or close associate had been seriously wounded in action. This occasion was no exception.

Figures in military uniform and in white smocks passed through the halls. The U.S. military hospital in Nuremburg was one of the largest medical establishments in Western Europe, and some of the best medical and surgical experts in the Army and the Air Force were stationed at the hospital. Brognola was grateful his fallen soldier had been moved here. The fighting men of Phoenix Force deserved the very best.

Captain Collins escorted Brognola to a private waiting room. Three men were seated in the room while a fourth paced the floor, occasionally puffing on a cigarette. Collins discreetly left Brognola with the others. The tall, fox-faced man on his feet was the first to shake hands with Brognola.

"Hello, David," the Fed announced. "I got here as quickly as I could."

"So did we," David McCarter replied grimly. "I hate this bloody waiting."

McCarter was a supertough Briton, raised in the rough-and-tumble East End of London. He was a veteran commando of the famous Special Air Service and had seen action in Southeast Asia, the mountains of Oman and the treacherous streets of Belfast. He had participated in Operation Nimrod, the successful SAS raid on the Iranian embassy in London. The Briton was a superb pilot, an Olympic-level pistol marksman and an expert in every form of combat.

McCarter was a man of action. He felt quite at home on the battlefield, but waiting made him surly and nervous. Patience had never been one of McCarter's virtues.

"What's the word on Rafael?" Brognola asked.

He referred to Rafael Encizo, the Cuban member of Phoenix Force. Encizo had been fighting oppression and injustice ever since he'd been a freedom fighter opposed to Castro's Communist regime. He survived the horrors of Castro's infamous political prison, El Principe, and escaped to the United States, where he had worked as a treasure hunter, diving instructor, professional bodyguard and insurance investigator before being recruited into Phoenix Force. The Cuban warrior was fearless in combat and fiercely loyal to his teammates. Rafael Encizo would willingly march into hell for the success of a mission.

And now, his life hung on a thread.

"He's alive," Colonel Yakov Katzenelenbogen told Brognola. "We're still waiting for the doctor's verdict."

Katz was middle-aged with a slight paunch and close-cropped iron-gray hair. His gentle blue eyes and polite manners suggested Yakov was a cultured man, intelligent, well educated and well traveled. In fact, these impressions were all correct, but Katz was also one of the most experienced and highly skilled fighting men in the world.

As a youth, Katz had fought in the Resistance against the Nazis in Europe before being drafted into service with the

American OSS and carrying out intelligence missions behind enemy lines. After the war, Katz moved to Palestine and joined the battle for the independence of the state of Israel. He later fought in the Six Day War, a conflict that cost Katz the life of his only son. Katz's right arm was damaged beyond repair by the same explosion that killed his son. The limb had to be amputated at the elbow, but this did not put Yakov Katzenelenbogen out of action.

Katz was an accomplished linguist who spoke six languages fluently. Added to his combat experience and clandestine skills, this made Katz one of the most valuable operatives in the shadowy world of espionage. In the Cold War, everything and everyone was a commodity. Katz was occasionally traded or loaned out to other intelligence networks. He worked with the American CIA, the British SIS, the French Sûreté and the West German BND.

With such an incredible background and extraordinary abilities, Yakov Katzenelenbogen was the perfect choice for unit commander of Phoenix Force.

"How badly is Rafael hurt?" Brognola inquired.

"A bullet creased his skull," Calvin James explained as he stretched his long legs and climbed out of a chair. "I wrapped his head to take care of external bleeding, but there wasn't much I could do about internal injuries. Any head wound has to be regarded as potentially dangerous."

A tall, athletic black man, James was the unit medic of Phoenix Force. He had learned most of his advanced medical skills as a hospital corpsman for the elite SEAL (Sea, Air and Land) unit in Vietnam. But James was already a veteran survivor before he joined the United States Navy. He was a product of the south side of Chicago where kids learn how to use their fists, feet and blades if they want to grow old enough to shave.

After Vietnam, James moved to California, planning to continue his study of medicine and chemistry on the GI Bill. However, when his sister and mother were killed by criminals, James decided to seek a career in law enforcement instead. He joined the San Francisco Police Department and soon became a member of the Special Weapons and Tactics unit. James was literally in the middle of a SWAT assignment when Phoenix Force drafted him for a mission against the sinister Black Alchemist terrorists. He had been part of Phoenix Force ever since.

"I was afraid he was already dead," Gary Manning remarked. "When I knelt beside him at the foot of the stairs and checked for a pulse, I was terrified I wouldn't find one."

Very little could terrify Gary Manning. The powerful, thickly muscled Canadian warrior was one of the best demolitions experts in the world and a superb rifle marksman. He served in Vietnam as a special observer attached to the Fifth Special Forces. After two years in Nam, Manning was unofficially assigned to the elite GSG-9 antiterrorist unit in West Germany.

A successful businessman as well as a security expert, champion long-distance runner and combat specialist, Manning attacked every task like a pit bull. His determination and stamina were matched only by his courage and skill. Manning was ideally suited to Phoenix Force.

No one appreciated the unique abilities and professionalism of these five warriors more than Hal Brognola. The Fed was the head honcho of Stony Man operations, a supersecret organization covertly created by executive order. The President of the United States had formed Stony Man to combat the growing threat of international terrorism. The challenge of these modern-day Vandal hordes had become too great to be dealt with by conventional law enforcement agencies or intelligence networks.

Stony Man was actually founded upon the incredible skills and combat experience of a single man—Mack Bolan, the Executioner. Bolan's one-man war with the Mafia was a twentieth-century legend. He had accomplished the impossible, pitting himself against the dragons of organized crime and emerging victorious. With Bolan for the hub of the organization and Brognola as the go-between for the Executioner and the Oval Office, Stony Man was created.

Phoenix Force's most recent mission had been in France where they crossed swords with a gang of terrorists controlled by ODESSA—the *Organisation der ehemaligen SS Angehörigen*. The Nazis were trying to revive the Third Reich, and their scheme had already cost the lives of a lot of innocent people before Phoenix Force arrived. The mission had been difficult and bloody, but successful. Yet the price of victory had been high. Rafael Encizo had fallen in the line of duty.

"I started up those stairs," Manning remarked grimly as he recalled how Encizo was wounded, "but Rafael insisted on going first. It should be me lying in that hospital bed instead of him."

"There's no reason to feel guilty about what happened, Gary," Katz told the Canadian. "The risk is part of the business. We've all known that from the start. What happened to Rafael could happen to any of us at any time."

"What kind of shape was Rafael in when you brought him here?" Brognola asked Calvin James.

"Comatose," the lanky black medic replied. "His pulse was weak, but steady. In a way, it was good that he didn't regain consciousness. It isn't safe to give a man any kind of medication when he's got a head wound until you can determine if there's been any brain damage. Neurosurgery is out of my line. This was the best hospital we could get him to in a hurry."

"A Colonel Towers is the surgeon in charge of Rafael's case," McCarter added, lighting another Player's cigarette. "All he's told us so far is that Rafael has suffered a concussion and a hairline fracture. A high-velocity bullet tends to do a bit of damage when it bounces off a chap's skull. Towers ordered a CAT scan to try to determine how bad the fracture is and whether there's been any brain damage."

"Last year we lost Keio," Manning said softly.

Keio Ohara had been one of the original five members of Phoenix Force. The tall Japanese electronics expert and martial artist had been killed in the final battle with the Black Alchemists. Ohara had been the first fatality among the elite commando unit. He had been the youngest of the five men, soft-spoken and polite, and a part of Phoenix had died with Keio Ohara.

Of course, the odds against surviving a mission were always slim. Eventually, every man in Phoenix Force would probably be killed in action. The five commandos were not frightened by this. In fact, they would all choose to fall on the battlefield rather than sit on the sidelines while others fought for the causes they believed in.

A short, middle-aged man with a balding skull entered the waiting room. He wore a silver eagle pinned to the lapel of his white smock. Colonel Towers nodded at the men who were eagerly awaiting his report concerning Encizo's condition.

"Sorry to take so long," the army surgeon began, looking at Brognola. "Is this your friend from Washington?"

"Ned Smithers," the Fed declared, using a cover name. "I'm with the Department of State."

"Uh-huh," Towers replied dryly. He did not believe Smithers was the guy's real name any more than he believed the other men were using their true identities. State Department? Bullshit. They were probably CIA or NSA or some other "sneaky Pete" outfit. "How's Ricardo?" Katz inquired, using Encizo's cover name.

"Your friend is tough," Colonel Towers answered. "Very tough. He's also lucky. You guys treated him for shock, correct?"

"That's right," James confirmed. "And infection and external bleeding."

"Good," Towers said with a nod. "Okay, the CAT scan didn't detect any brain damage. Computerized axial tomography is sort of a color X-ray that gives more details than we'd have otherwise. The skull fractured in a clean break.

No bone splinters reached the brain. The electroencephalogram didn't detect anything irregular in the brain waves either, so it doesn't appear the concussion has caused any damage.''

"Thank God," Manning said with relief.

"Well, your friend isn't out of the woods yet," Towers warned. "He's still in a coma and the longer he remains in that condition, the greater the chance of lack of oxygen to the blood, which can result in brain damage. First, we have to prepare him for surgery to take care of that fracture. Then we'll see what can be done about the coma."

"What are his chances, Colonel?" Katz asked, pulling a cigarette from a pack of Camels, using the steel hooks at the end of the prosthesis attached to the stump of his right arm.

"I can't make any promises," Towers answered, "but Ricardo is in excellent physical condition. His lungs are very strong and his heart is in perfect shape. I'd say he's got better than a sixty percent chance of a full recovery."

"Full recovery?" Brognola raised his eyebrows. "Does that mean mentally as well as physically?"

"Do you want to know if he'll still be able to do whatever you've been putting him through in the past?" the doctor asked with a sneer in his voice. "That man's got more scar tissue on his body than most of the guys we stitched back together in Nam. Did you know he'd been tortured? The scars are at least twenty years old, but the cause is unmistakable. Looks like somebody used his testicles for an ashtray."

"Thought you were concerned with Ricardo's skull, Doctor," McCarter commented.

"How long do you think you can keep putting a man through that sort of punishment? Even if his body recovers, his mind is bound to carry psychological scars for the rest of his life—"

"Doctor," Brognola cut him off abruptly. "My men aren't indentured servants. Any of them can quit anytime they want. God knows that man you've examined doesn't need to prove his courage to anyone. He's done that a thousand times in ways you couldn't begin to imagine. I'm not going to pressure him to make any decisions one way or the other, but I won't insult him by judging how he should live, either. You just concentrate on taking care of him, Colonel. I want that man to receive the very best of care.''

"That's one thing I can promise, Mr. Smithers,'' Towers assured him.

"I know, Colonel,'' the Fed agreed. "You're the best neurosurgeon in the West. That's why we wanted you to handle Ricardo.''

"You've got me,'' Towers stated. "Now, I'd better get back to my patient. And you fellas ought to get some rest. Leave a phone number where I can get in touch when we know more. Okay?''

"Of course, Doctor,'' Brognola answered. "And thank you.''

As the surgeon headed into the corridor, Brognola turned to the four members of Phoenix Force. They all felt a common loss. The brotherhood of Stony Man was deep, the brotherhood of men bound together by dedication to a common cause and mutual respect.

"Well, shit,'' the Fed muttered. "I understand the mission in France went pretty well except for what happened to Rafael.''

"We'll make a full report on the mission later, Hal,'' Katz replied. "ODESSA turned out to be behind that mess. The Nazis will be licking their wounds for quite a while, I'm happy to say.''

"The report can wait,'' Brognola assured him. "You guys better check into a hotel here in Nuremburg and try to get some sleep. I'm going to have a talk with the hospital administrator before I head back to Stony Man. Able Team is currently involved in another mission, so I can't stay here and wait for—''

"Mr. Smithers!" Captain Collins called as he ran through the corridor to the waiting room. "Mr. Smithers, you received an urgent telephone call from the President!"

"On a direct line?" Brognola frowned, only mildly surprised by the announcement. "Are you sure it isn't a hoax?"

"I don't think so, sir," the captain replied. "But it's sure a strange message."

"What sort of message?" the Fed asked.

"The President wants you to turn on a television set on the double, sir," Collins answered. "He said to watch the news and you'll know what to do next."

3

The four members of Phoenix Force and the Stony Man commander switched on a small black-and-white TV set in the waiting room. The American Forces Network news was already in progress. An all-too-familiar scene of a riot appeared on the screen. The violence was relatively mild, but the real story concerned the fate of two American VIPs in the Republic of South Africa.

"The riot occurred during Senator Finley's speech," a reporter's voice declared as the film footage continued. "Johannesburg police and soldiers quickly subdued the crowd, and this is when the kidnapping allegedly occurred. An unidentified American camera crew filmed this vehicle leaving the area."

The picture froze briefly, and a white circle appeared around a Hippo van hurrying from the scene. As the film footage of the riot ended, a photogenic news reporter with wavy hair and a lantern jaw appeared on the screen. He wore a pressed, white bush shirt and held a cordless microphone in his fist as he stood before a large concrete and glass building.

"The South African government claims to have no information about the kidnapping," the reporter said, staring grimly into the camera. "They claim the vehicle, an army Hippo, was stolen and the three soldiers assigned to the van were later found bound and gagged. The government is blaming this abduction on the antiapartheid forces. However, Edward Nommo, a spokesman for the United

Democratic Front, denies this charge and insists the government must be responsible. All that's certain at this moment is Reverend Robert Lincoln and Senator Tom Finley are missing and no one seems to know where they are, why they were kidnapped or whether they're alive or dead."

The reporter allowed a dramatic pause before he added, "I'm Kenneth Walterson, in Johannesburg."

Brognola switched off the television set. "I think we can guess what the President wants us to do now," he commented.

"Yeah," Gary Manning muttered. "The impossible."

"That's sort of our specialty, isn't it?" David McCarter asked with a grin. The Briton's mood always improved when he sensed Phoenix Force was about to go into action.

"The mission is obvious," Katzenelenbogen remarked. "The President wants us to go to South Africa and rescue Lincoln and Finley."

"If they're not dead already," Calvin James added. "Shit, Hal. How are we supposed to carry out a mission in South Africa? We can't expect much cooperation from the government. For all we know, the government had those dudes bagged. Besides, I'm not real eager to go to a country that practices racial discrimination as part of its national policies. Not the sort of place I'd pick for a vacation, if you know what I mean."

"It won't be a vacation for any of you," Brognola stated. "And you don't have to take the assignment if you object to it, Cal. If Able Team manages to wrap up their current mission in time, I'll send them instead."

"We can't wait that long," Katz declared. "The more time we waste, the less chance we have of finding Lincoln and Finley alive."

"But we'll need some sort of contacts down there," Manning said. "And we don't know who to trust."

"What's new about that?" McCarter inquired. "We've had lots of missions where we couldn't trust anyone."

"But we've always had some sort of contacts," Manning insisted. "Even one of your buddies involved in gunrunning or the black market would be better than nothing. You have any old associates like that in South Africa, David?"

"Not that I know of," the Briton answered. "But some of those blokes get around quite a bit, running from country to country and such."

"Well," James began, "the Johannesburg bigwigs aren't going to welcome us with open arms—especially *me*. There's at least a fifty-fifty chance they kidnapped those dudes. The South African government isn't exactly squeaky clean."

"What government is?" Brognola replied. "Look, Cal, I don't claim to be an authority on South Africa, but the government agreed to let Lincoln and Finley into the country. They allowed those guys to conduct public speeches in front of TV cameras. They must have suspected Finley and Lincoln would bad-mouth the government and apartheid, but as far as I could tell, there was no attempt to censor them."

"You didn't see enough of the broadcast to know that," James said.

"I saw the ABC *Nightline* programs that were broadcast from Johannesburg," McCarter stated. "They had interviews with President Botha and Bishop Tutu. Both the government and the apartheid dissidents were able to speak their views. Say what you want about South Africa, they didn't have to agree to that broadcast. Even Ted Koppel admitted he saw little evidence of censorship by the government, either of ABC or of local press criticisms of the government."

"Don't tell me you approve of apartheid, David?" James glared at the Briton.

"Of course not, mate," McCarter assured him. "My point is, South Africa isn't on a level with the Soviet Union or Libya when it comes to censorship and discrimination. Also, they're obviously trying to appear to be more tolerant in order to improve their image abroad."

"Which is why they let Lincoln and Finley into the country," Brognola added. "Why risk shooting that image to hell by kidnapping those two? If the government had arranged the abduction, they wouldn't use an army Hippo and grab Lincoln and Finley right in front of TV cameras."

"Maybe not," James said with a shrug. "And maybe they're using reverse logic. Just because South Africa allowed American television to broadcast from Johannesburg doesn't prove much. Last year the *Today Show* broadcast from Moscow for a whole week."

"That's true," Katz stated. "But Moscow only allowed members of the Communist Party to be interviewed. The only critics of the Kremlin spoke to the Soviets via satellite connection. No dissidents living in the Soviet Union were included. However, Bishop Tutu and other opponents of apartheid still live in South Africa, so Botha's regime must not be as oppressive as the Kremlin."

"So you're ready to blame the kidnapping on the anti-apartheid forces?" James stared at Katz. "Israel and South Africa are allies, aren't they, Yakov?"

"Hey," Manning said quickly. "Let's not get in a big quarrel about this—"

"Just a minute," Katz urged. "I'm a Jew, Calvin, and thus I'm an Israeli. I'm also a naturalized American citizen. In a sense, Phoenix Force allows me to fight for the interests of both nations as well as the rest of the free world."

"I didn't mean to question your loyalty, Yakov," James assured him. "But I can't say I'm thrilled that Israel and South Africa are buddies."

"Israel and South Africa have certain things in common," Katz admitted. "Both countries are currently threatened by communism. That's not paranoia. It happens to be fact. Angola, Zambia, Somalia, Mozambique and Ethopia are all Marxist or neo-Marxist regimes. Zimbabwe claims to be a democracy, but Robert Mugabe is a Marxist socialist tied to the Soviet Union as well. Farther north are Libya, Algeria, Ghana, Togo and the small Communist state of Benin. All of these African countries are hostile toward both Israel and South Africa. I might add, with the possible exception of Zimbabwe, all are also one-party dictatorships, but very little is said about their disregard for human rights. Israel and South Africa are allies due to a desire for self-preservation.''

"Wait a minute," Manning said. "I remember reading that Zimbabwe had established new diplomatic relations with South Africa.''

"*New* relations indeed," Katz confirmed. "Mugabe broke off diplomatic relations with South Africa in 1980, but discovered his country's economy couldn't continue without trade relations with South Africa, a fact he was no doubt embarrassed to admit.''

"I still don't like apartheid," James insisted.

"Neither do I," Katz assured him. "But we can't let that blind us to the fact that the South African government wouldn't be stupid enough to kidnap Lincoln and Finley. That doesn't exclude the possibility that extremists *within* the government or the military might be responsible.''

"Which means we can expect a certain amount of cooperation from the government," McCarter mused. "But we can't really trust them. Business as usual, eh?''

"Okay," Brognola began. "Time's a'wasting. You guys want the job or not?''

"Yeah," James said with a shrug. "Somebody's gotta do it.''

"I'll try to cut through the usual red tape and arrange some sort of contacts for you in South Africa," the Fed declared. "The President is probably already working on that, but I'll make sure it's taken care of. I'll also arrange a military flight for you guys. Shouldn't be too difficult since there are a lot of U.S. Army and Air Force bases in West Germany. I just wish Encizo was able to join you. I don't like sending you guys on a mission with a team member missing.''

"Maybe we can get a replacement for this mission," Katz suggested. "An ideal man for the job may be available right here in Germany."

"You have somebody special in mind?" Brognola asked.

"Yes," the Israeli replied. "Somebody we've worked with before."

"Of course," McCarter said. "Karl Hahn."

"I remember now," Brognola declared, snapping his fingers. "The BND agent you fellas worked with during that mission in Turkey a while back."

"Hahn is a good man," Gary Manning stated. "He was trained as an antiterrorist when he was in the GSG-9. Besides being a first-class commando, Hahn is also an electronics expert and a computer whiz."

"Yeah," James added. "The dude also has a real talent for improvising weapons in hand-to-hand combat. Hahn can kill with a rolled-up newspaper or a pocket bomb. Anything he can get his hands on, Hahn can use as a weapon."

"I remember reading something about that in the file we've got on Hahn back at Stony Man," Brognola recalled. "Hahn would be an ideal replacement for Rafael, *if* we can get him."

"Karl said he was going to be transferred back to the Federal Republic of Germany," McCarter said. "That was some time ago. Hopefully he hasn't been shipped out of the country on another assignment."

"And hopefully we can persuade BND to let us borrow Hahn for a while," Manning remarked.

"Don't worry," Brognola assured him. "If Hahn is in Germany, I'll get him for you."

4

Karl Hahn shook his head with despair as he read the passage from *The Two Gentlemen of Verona* for the third time.

" 'Yet writers say,' " Hahn read aloud, " 'as in the sweetest bud the eating canker dwells, so eating love inhabits in the finest wits of all.' "

Hahn uttered an exasperated sigh. "Now, what the hell does that mean?"

Hahn had recently completed an assignment for the Bundesnachrichtendienst, the West German equivalent of the American CIA. The mission had been a rather routine surveillance operation, following the activities of a couple of East German agents who were trying to gather information about the NATO defense systems within the Federal Republic. The Communist operatives tried to bribe some army officers to give them classified information, but only one lieutenant accepted the bribe, and the East Germans were promptly arrested along with their traitorous ally.

The mission had been simple and relatively dull. It had also taken three long months to produce results. Most intelligence work is more cloak than dagger. It requires time and patience. The tension and concentration involved is very demanding. Hahn had been given a two-week vacation at the end of the mission.

Hahn took advantage of the free time to visit the Bienenkorb Library in Bonn. The BND agent understood four languages fluently, and the Bienenkorb had an excellent selection of foreign language books, including numerous volumes in English. Hahn had selected the works of the most celebrated playwright in the English language, William Shakespeare. Studying the bard seemed an ideal way to improve his English.

The idea worked better in theory than practice. Hahn soon discovered that Shakespearean English was quite different from the language he had learned as an exchange student in California. He had to constantly check the glossary at the rear of the book in order to make head or tail of what he read.

Hahn decided to try a different play. He leafed through the pages to *Hamlet*, possibly Shakespeare's most famous work.

"'Nay, answer me. Stand and unfold yourself,'" Hahn read the second verse from Act One aloud. "Sounds like a flasher," he muttered. Just then, two men strolled into the English language section. Hahn glanced up at the pair. Both were young and dressed in ill-treated trousers, wrinkled jackets and pullover shirts. One fellow's hair was jet black and extended to his shoulder blades. His companion had close-cropped straw-colored hair. It was bleached from exposure to the sun, so pale one might mistake the owner as bald from a distance.

Hahn could not see their features clearly. Both men were turned toward the bookshelves, examining the volumes of Dickens and Sir Arthur Conan Doyle. The pair seemed to be avoiding looking directly at Hahn, but they slowly moved closer to his table.

As the BND agent closed the thick volume of Shakespeare and began to rise from his chair, the two men charged. Each held a dagger in his fist, cheap replicas of the Fairbairn-Sykes commando knife, with six-inch blades.

Hahn raised his book in both hands as the long-haired assailant lunged forward. The knife struck the leather-bound cover and the steel tip stabbed into the surface. Hahn felt the impact of the blow ride through his hands and arms.

He quickly bent an elbow and swung it into the side of his attacker's face.

Long Hair stumbled backward with a groan. The dagger was still stuck in the book as Hahn turned toward the second assailant. Blondie handled a knife better than his hairy partner. He kept his blade low as he swung a sly thrust, trying to drive it under Hahn's rib cage.

Hahn swatted the book across the knife jockey's fist. Blondie yelped as his hand popped open and the knife dropped from his grasp. The blow also jarred the other dagger loose from the Shakespeare volume, and it fell to the floor at Hahn's feet as the BND man adroitly rammed a corner of the book into Blondie's solar plexus.

The would-be assassin gasped, his breath exploding from his open mouth. Hahn quickly thrust his arms forward and drove the sturdy spine of the book under the man's jawbone, sending the killer staggering backward. As the attacker dropped to his knees, stunned by the blow, Hahn closed in fast and hammered the book spine against the base of his opponent's skull. Blondie moaned and fell unconscious.

The long-haired goon had been dazed by Hahn's elbow smash, but he was still on his feet. He had hesitated too long to come to the assistance of his partner, and he did not intend to tangle with Karl Hahn with his bare hands. The killer reached inside his jacket and drew a Czech M-1950 pistol from his belt.

Hahn saw the gun and hurled the Shakespeare volume at his opponent. The book hit Long Hair on the upper arm as he started to point his pistol, distracting the gunman and knocking his aim off target as he pulled the trigger.

A 7.65 mm projectile hissed past Hahn's right cheek. He thought he felt something nip his earlobe and a bolt of icy fear shot up his spine. No sane man is immune to fear, but Hahn had learned to channel it into his muscles and reflexes without allowing panic to make him reckless or clumsy.

Hahn quickly grabbed the backrest of his chair as the startled gunman tried to aim his weapon once more. Pivoting away from the table, Hahn swung the chair in a fast, desperate sweep. The wooden legs crashed into Long Hair's forearm and chest, and the blow knocked the pistol from the man's hand and sent him hurtling backward into the nearest bookcase.

The BND agent snapped a karate kick to his assailant's gut, and as the killer doubled up Hahn quickly grabbed a fistful of stringy black hair. He pulled hard and hauled the aggressor forward, shoving his opponent into the table. Long Hair shrieked when his groin connected with the corner of the furniture.

Hahn moved behind his opponent and pushed hard. Long Hair fell across the tabletop. The BND agent seized the assassin's head, using his ears for handles, as he slammed the man's face into the hard wood surface. He repeated this ruthless tactic twice more to be certain his opponent was unconscious.

"Was ist das . . . ?" a woman's voice began.

A librarian had left her desk to investigate the unruly noise coming from the English book section. The lady's eyes widened with horror behind her horn-rimmed glasses when she saw Karl Hahn and the two senseless bodies of his opponents.

"Guten Tag, Fräulein," the BND man said with a shrug.

"Ach, Gott!" The librarian gasped, backing away from the scene.

Suddenly, a man appeared beside the woman, holding a compact Skorpion machine pistol. The librarian screamed, and the gunman struck her across the chest with a forearm and sent her crashing to the floor. He quickly aimed the Skorpion at Karl Hahn.

The BND agent had already ducked behind the table and reached inside his suit jacket to draw a Walther P-5 pistol from shoulder leather. The gunman triggered his Czech blaster and copper-jacketed 7.65 mm rounds splintered the tabletop above Hahn.

Two stray bullets punched into the long-haired man, who lay across the table. Another slug struck the floor inches from Karl Hahn's left knee. The BND agent slithered under the table and rose up alongside the heavy furniture.

The man with the Skorpion hadn't noticed Hahn had moved to a different position. The BND pro snap-aimed his Walther and squeezed off two shots. Both 9 mm Parabellum rounds crashed into the gunman's chest, and the Skorpion dropped from the killer's hands as he tumbled lifeless to the floor.

Yet another gunman appeared in the English section, and as this new assailant swung a Soviet-made PPS submachine gun at Hahn, the BND agent ducked behind the table once more. He waited for the metallic chatter of a full-auto weapon, but no sound erupted from his opponent's death machine.

Hahn chanced a look and saw a steel hook slash across the gunsel's wrist, striking the man's hand from the grips and trigger of the Russian music box. The killer screamed as the metal claw ripped cloth and bit into his flesh. The subgun fell to the floor.

Colonel Yakov Katzenelenbogen rammed the prosthesis attached to the stump of his right arm, punching the curved steel of his hooks into the man's solar plexus. The gunman doubled up with a breathless gasp. Katz's left hand grabbed the guy's hair, and he jerked the fellow's head downward and slammed a knee under the gunman's jaw. The invader sagged in Katz's grasp, and the Phoenix Force warrior shoved the senseless figure aside.

"Gott im Himmel," Karl Hahn whispered, lowering his pistol. "What are you doing here, Yakov?"

"Looking for you," Katz replied. "I'll explain later. Who are your playmates, Karl?"

"We didn't get around to introductions," Hahn answered, "but I suspect these fellows are probably with the

Red Army faction. They've been upset with me for killing some of their comrades a while back. I heard rumors the terrorists had a contract out for me. Guess it must be true.''

"Popularity can be a bitch," Calvin James commented as he joined Katz and Hahn. "How are you doing, Karl? Doesn't look like the bastards nailed you."

"They came close," the BND man answered, placing a finger to his earlobe. It was wet and Hahn was surprised to see blood. The enemy's bullet *had* nicked his ear, after all.

Katz helped the librarian rise from the floor. "Are you hurt, *Fräulein*?" he asked in German.

"Nein, mein Herr," she replied, assuring him she was all right. *"Danke, mein Herr."*

The Israeli nodded and turned his attention back to Hahn. "As I recall, the German Red Army faction usually has more than one backup for a hit."

"That's right," the BND man confirmed. "You fellows might have arrived in time for round two."

"Aren't we lucky?" Calvin James muttered.

AS IF TO PROVE Hahn was correct, two terrorists burst through the front door of the library. A female savage with dirty blond hair plastered on her head carried a Skorpion machine pistol. Her male comrade was armed with a Heckler & Koch MP-5. Fortunately, the innocent bystanders in the library had been alerted to danger by Hahn's battle with the first three attackers. Most of them were still crouched behind tables and desks when the new threat arrived.

"Schweinhund!" the woman terrorist snarled as she opened fire with the Skorpion.

Several 7.65 mm slugs raked a tabletop where two hapless college students were huddled low. One student managed to duck fast enough to avoid the spray of 90-grain projectiles. The other received a stray round through the forehead and another bullet under the right eye socket. His head bounced from the impact, a pink mist spraying from the back of his skull. The student collapsed and graduated to the realm of the dead.

Gary Manning had stationed himself by a bookcase near the front entrance. He drew an Eagle autoloader from the shoulder holster under his sport jacket and aimed the big steel pistol carefully. He squeezed the trigger. A .357 round catapulted from the muzzle of Manning's Israeli-made Magnum. The big 158-grain wadcutter smashed into the female terrorist's chest, drilling through her left breast to blast her black heart. The bitch howled as the Magnum punch hurled her back through the doorway. Her lifeless body tumbled outside and rolled down the front steps of the library.

The remaining terrorist swung his H&K machine gun toward Manning's position. He hadn't noticed David McCarter stationed by the metal cabinets of the card index files. The British fighting ace held his Browning Hi-Power in a two-hand Weaver's combat grip. McCarter triggered two rounds and both 9 mm slugs struck the terrorist in the side of the head. The gunman's skull split open, brains splashing from shattered bone. The Red Army flunky was dead before his body hit the floor.

"Better check the back door," Karl Hahn told Katz and James, gesturing toward the rear of the library with his Walther P-5 pistol.

"You two take care of that," Katz replied. "I'll see if our friends need any help up front."

"Gotcha," Calvin James agreed as he pulled a Colt Combat Commander from the holster under his left arm.

Hahn headed for the back door with James at his heels, reaching the rear exit as two Red Army freaks entered. The first terrorist cursed under his breath and swung the sawed-off barrels of an Italian shotgun at the BND agent and the black Phoenix Force warrior.

Hahn's Walther and James's Colt roared before the terrorist could trigger his over-under blaster. A 115-grain Parabellum tore into his upper lip, shattering the gunman's upper jaw and driving bone shards into his brain. The big .45 slug hit the terrorist's chest at the same instant, crashing his sternum and tearing into his heart.

The double-dead fanatic dropped to the floor, shotgun still unfired in his frozen grip. The second terrorist retreated through the door to the alley outside, where he took a Soviet F-1 hand grenade from a pocket, pulled the pin and tossed the grenade at the two warriors before slamming the door shut.

"Shit!" James exclaimed as he scooped up the grenade and hastily hurled it at the door.

The deadly sphere shattered the window of the top panel of the door. James and Hahn immediately dropped to the floor and covered their heads with their arms. The F-1 blaster exploded in the alley, and the door burst off its hinges and crashed to the floor. The bloodied, pulverized remnants of the last terrorist were splattered all over the alley, scattered with other forms of garbage spilled from the trash cans he had cowered behind.

"Are you all right?" Katz called as he approached James and Hahn.

"Yeah," James replied. "Fella almost wasted us, but I managed to throw him a curve."

"*Scheisser,*" Hahn muttered, rubbing the side of his head. "I wish I'd brought some earplugs."

"Did we get all of these sons of bitches, Yakov?" James asked as he climbed to his feet and returned the Colt Commander to shoulder leather.

"Yes," the Phoenix Force commander confirmed. "Unfortunately, a citizen was killed by the terrorists as well."

"Are you sure the fella's dead?" James inquired, reaching for a small medical kit at the small of his back.

"I'm sure," Katz replied. "I'm afraid there's nothing you can do for him, my friend."

"I'm grateful you fellows came to my aid," Hahn began. "And I'm very glad to see you again, but I don't think you just happened to be passing by and decided to stop by the library for a little light reading.''

"We've got a mission, Karl,'' Katz explained. "Rafael is in the hospital and we need a reliable replacement.''

"You've got me,'' Hahn reassured him.

"That's the lot of them,'' McCarter called out. "We checked outside and didn't find any more bastards lurking about.''

"Shh, man,'' James said, holding a finger to his lips. "After all, you should keep the noise down while you're in a library.''

5

The Bundesnachrichtendienst convinced the Bonn police that the incident at the Bienenkorb Library had simply been a vicious terrorist act that had been dealt with by the BND and certain "Interpol agents" interested in the case. Details about this were, of course, classified as a matter of national security. The BND did not want the police to inconvenience their allies simply because a few people had been killed.

The police, for their part, agreed to turn the matter over to the BND. The Federal Republic of Germany has seen more than its share of terrorist activity. The Bonn police had tangled with every lunatic group from the Baader-Meinhoff Gang to the Turkish Gray Wolves. They were perfectly willing to let the BND and Interpol take full responsibility for the investigation of the library incident.

Arrangements had already been made for Karl Hahn's special assignment with Phoenix Force. Hal Brognola's Stony Man connections allowed him to get a military transport ready for the five warriors' trip to South Africa.

When Phoenix Force arrived at the Jan Smuts International Airport, they emerged from the C-130 and hauled out their gear. Three men stood by a Hippo van parked near the runway and calmly waited for the five strangers. Two members of the reception committee wore khaki uniform. The third wore a light tan suit with a white shirt open at the throat.

"Hello, gentlemen," the man in the suit said as Phoenix Force drew closer. "I am Pieter van Schooer from the Ministry of Internal Security. Welcome to the Republic of South Africa.''

The tone of van Schooer's voice was formal and a bit curt. His accent as well as his name suggested the man was an Afrikaner. Not all whites in South Africa were Afrikaners, but the Afrikaners had lived in the country since 1652. Largely of Dutch and German descent, they settled in the region before most of the black tribes that currently reside in South Africa. Only the Hottentots and the Bushmen can claim to be original natives.

The Afrikaners, formerly known as Boers, were the ruling class of South Africa. Their ancestors had fought the Zulu and later the British to hold on to their claim to the land.

"This is Captain Whitney and Sergeant Muspula of the Bureau of Security Services," van Schooer said, introducing his companions.

Captain Whitney was a well-built young white man with straw-blond hair and gray eyes. His sun-tanned face offered a wide smile as he nodded at the men of Phoenix Force. Sergeant Muspula, a wiry black man with a lean ebony face, did not display any sort of welcome. Sunglasses concealed his eyes, but each man of Phoenix Force suspected Muspula was probably glaring at them.

Phoenix Force loaded their gear into the Hippo and Sergeant Muspula moved behind the wheel of the vehicle, while the other men took their seats in the rear of the armor-plated van. Muspula switched on the engine and the Hippo lurched forward.

"As instructed by my superiors," van Schooer began, "we shall avoid customs."

He glanced at the bulky aluminum cases and canvas duffel bags the visitors had loaded into the Hippo. Van Schooer wondered what sort of gear the mysterious strangers carried, but he didn't bother to ask. Captain Whitney was more open with his curiosity.

"You chaps have firearms packed away?" the captain inquired. Unlike van Schooer's, Whitney's accent resembled that of an Englishman from Manchester. "You know, you can bring guns legally into South Africa as long as you've got proof of legal ownership and all the serial numbers are clearly stamped on the weapons. Of course, you have to get a permit while you're in the country, but that's not much of a problem."

"Our equipment is rather unusual," Katzenelenbogen replied. "Not the sort of thing we care to bring through customs."

"Indeed," van Schooer remarked. "I thought you fellows were CIA investigators or something like that. What do you need weapons for?"

"In case investigating turns up some results," Gary Manning replied simply.

"Actually," Katz stated, "we're not investigators. We'll help gather intelligence and access information all right, but that isn't our specialty."

"Oh?" Van Schooer raised his bushy eyebrows. "And what *is* your specialty, Mr. . . . ?"

"Just call me Wallburg," Katz replied.

"I see." The Afrikaner sighed. "You fellows are using false names. How droll."

"Glad you like it," McCarter said dryly.

"Your specialty, Mr. Wallburg?" Captain Whitney urged.

"Seek and destroy," Katz told him. "But first we have to make certain we have the right target. In this case, we have to find out who kidnapped Senator Finley and Reverend Lincoln."

"We know who's responsible," van Schooer declared. "It was the United Democratic Union or some other group of radicals. Perhaps the outlawed South African Communist Party."

"Or SWAPO," Sergeant Muspula commented without taking his eyes from the windshield. "That's the so-called South-West Africa People's Organization. Those damned terrorists are based in Angola. The Communists send them into Bophuthatswana, Namibia and other black sovereign nations that maintain friendly relations with South Africa. Those goddamn Ovimbundu and Bakongo trash from Angola seldom have the nerve to take direct action in South Africa, but those kaffir boot-lickers follow orders from the Cubans and the Soviets in Angola. If Moscow ordered a kidnapping, those kaffirs would do it for them."

"What's a kaffir?" Manning asked.

"It's the Afrikaner equivalent of nigger," Calvin James answered. "Sounds kind of funny coming from you, Sergeant."

"Black Africans are not all alike," Muspula told him. "Any stupid savage who endorses communism is a kaffir as far as I'm concerned."

"Yeah," James mused. "Well, maybe there wouldn't have been a Communist takeover of Angola if the Portuguese rule had been less oppressive. Just like there would be less criticism toward South Africa if the government did away with apartheid."

"You think it would be that simple?" Muspula laughed. "You American blacks are really amusing. You think because your ancestors came from Africa you understand this continent? You think you understand the Zulu, the Xphoso, the Hottentots or any of the other black tribes who live in South Africa? Many of them are traditional enemies who would slaughter each other if apartheid did not exist."

"Which gives the folks in power a reason to continue the practice," James snorted.

"We're tired of the way you Americans and the British and the United Nations are always meddling in our affairs and telling South Africa how to run its own country," van Schooer stated. "None of you lofty moralists seem very upset by the Communist regimes of Angola or Mozambique. Zaire is a dictatorship with an extremely high poverty level and terribly low standard of living for the two hundred Bantu tribes that live under that tyranny. Yet President Seko is listed as one of the wealthiest men in the world. But the U.N. never criticizes these countries, and the Americans and the British never voice protests about human-rights violations by these regimes."

"I recall a former U.S. ambassador named Andrew Young," Captain Whitney added. "He once said the Cubans had brought 'stability' to Angola. Ha! Stability from the barrel of their AK-47s! The Cubans and the Russians are still running Angola, you know. They'll take over the entire continent of Africa if we let them. Look what happened in Rhodesia. Look what's happening in Namibia today! The U.N. criticizes South Africa because we haven't granted Namibia independence. Yet we've promised to do this as soon as the Soviets and the Cubans pull out of Namibia. The U.N. wants us to grant independence immediately, but they don't object to the Communists occupying Namibia. Do you think this is fair or logical or even bloody rational?"

"That's the United Nations," McCarter said with a shrug. "They've never protested the Soviet involvement in Afghanistan or Poland either, but they cried bloody blue murder about Britain's actions in the Falklands and the Americans in Grenada."

"Look," Katz said evenly. "We didn't come here to debate politics. We've got a job to do and that's all we're concerned with at the moment."

"I assure you," van Schooer began, "everything possible is being done to try to locate Senator Finley and Reverend Lincoln. After all, it's been less than forty-eight hours since they were kidnapped."

"Everything?" Karl Hahn remarked. "It seems to me you've already decided either an antiapartheid group or the Communists are guilty. Have you even considered the possibility someone within the government might be responsible?''

"That's absurd," van Schooer replied. "Perhaps you've already decided to condemn us. Americans are very fond of accusing South Africa of everything they can think of. After all, Finley and Lincoln never traveled to any other African countries to protest unfair policies. They never visited the Soviet Union or Cambodia to complain about the outright genocide taking place in those countries. Of course, I shouldn't be surprised. Idi Amin was in power in Uganda for six years and slaughtered more than three hundred thousand of his own people before America or Amnesty International made any criticisms about that lunatic."

"And little was said about the Obote regime, which had massacred about a hundred thousand after he took over Uganda," Captain Whitney added.

"Calm down, gentlemen," Katz urged. "We're not accusing your government of kidnapping. However, certain extremists in government or among the white minority may have been involved in the abduction of Lincoln and Finley. I'm certain their speeches didn't overwhelm most Afrikaners with joy."

"You blokes might be right that South Africa has been getting a lot of bad press while regimes that may be far worse are getting very little criticism," McCarter commented. "But the fact is, fair or unfair, you've got a pretty bad public image these days. It won't get any better if we fail to find Finley and Lincoln."

"They may already be dead," van Schooer said. "There haven't been any ransom demands. No statements allegedly made by the pair have been sent to the government or the press. No group has claimed responsibility for the abduction."

"I'd be surprised if they had," Hahn commented. "If the kidnappers are opposed to the South African government, they're probably hoping you fellows will be blamed for the incident."

"And if somebody inside the government is responsible," James added, "they're probably hoping you'll crack down on the antiapartheid groups."

"And if the Communists are behind it," Katz declared, "they're probably hoping *both* reactions will occur. That would leave this country very vulnerable for a revolution, almost certainly with the Marxist forces from Angola and Mozambique jumping into the battle."

"Then you appreciate the threat of communism to South Africa?" van Schooer asked with surprise.

"I appreciate the fact that the Soviets would love to get control of South Africa," Katz confirmed. "This country is one of the greatest sources of diamonds, manganese ore, uranium and chromium in the world. Of course, South Africa is also the largest supplier of gold. The Soviets are in second place in that department, and it would be a very valuable feather in the Kremlin's hat if they could seize control of two thirds of the gold production of the entire world."

"So where do we begin?" Manning wondered aloud.

"Speculation without facts is useless," Katz declared. "We'll need to evaluate every scrap of information."

"You'll have access to everything you'll need when we reach Johannesburg," van Schooer promised.

SERGEANT MUSPULA DROVE the Hippo along Harrow Street in the Yeoville section of Johannesburg. Eventually, the Hippo pulled into an alley next to a television repair shop, and the men climbed out of the vehicle and entered the building via a side door. They stepped inside a storage room filled with crates and aluminum shelves loaded with cardboard boxes.

"This is our safe house, which will be used as the base of operations while you're in South Africa," van Schooer explained. "The security here is very tight. Only the individuals in this building know the exact location of this safe house. Not even the president or the director of the BSS have this information."

"Driving up in an armored military vehicle isn't exactly discreet, Mr. van Schooer," Hahn said.

"It's not terribly suspicious either," the Afrikaner assured him. "Not with the amount of trouble we've had in South Africa lately."

"The natives are restless," Calvin James muttered as he placed a duffel bag on the floor.

"I was referring to the tension caused by the kidnapping of Finley and Lincoln," van Schooer declared.

"That's why we're here," Katz said with a nod.

"Did you people install a computer here?" Hahn inquired, stripping off his jacket to reveal the Walther P-5 in shoulder leather under his left arm. "I need a terminal with access to the main memory banks of your intelligence computers in order to collect and evaluate information."

"No," van Schooer admitted, "but we can arrange that."

"We can kick around a few things before the high-tech equipment arrives," Manning remarked. "What do you guys have so far?"

"We believe the most likely suspects in this case are militant branches of the antiapartheid movement," van Schooer replied. "I'm sorry if that upsets you."

"You might be right," James was forced to admit. "I seem to recall that a gang of extremists murdered a number of blacks who support the government a while back. If I remember right, they hacked their victims to death with knives and set fire to the remains."

"Last year forty militants also dragged a chap out of his car, doused him with lighter fluid and set him afire," Captain Whitney added. "You see, all the antiapartheid blokes aren't the sweet, gentle people your media thinks they are."

"I don't agree with apartheid," James stated, "but I don't approve of terror tactics either."

"Glad to hear that," van Schooer commented. "At any rate, we think an extremist element within the United Democratic Front might be responsible for the kidnappings. Possibly a splinter group calling itself FASA—Free All South Africans.''

"Any particular reason to suspect them?'' Katz inquired.

"It's a new organization and we don't have much information about them so far,'' van Schooer confessed. "But we know they've got caches of weapons tucked away, and they've been quite outspoken about changing the current rule in South Africa by any means possible, including violence.''

"Of course, Bishop Tutu has indicated that he wouldn't rule out violence either,'' Whitney added. "I know he received a Nobel Peace Prize, but Tutu has long been connected with the African National Congress, which most non-Communist Africans regard as a terrorist organization.''

"The Nazis felt the same way about the French Resistance,'' James commented dryly.

"You'd compare my government to the Nazis?'' Van Schooer glared at James.

"I wouldn't,'' Katz interrupted. "And I fought the Nazis in Europe. Hitler's legions didn't include Jewish soldiers, but there are blacks in the South African army and among the police officers of your cities. Your government has actually lifted a number of the restrictions against blacks, including the right to form their own labor unions. The Nazis would never have permitted something like that.''

"South Africa still has a lot of changes to make before it gets an A-for-equality in my book,'' James insisted. "But the FASA might be a terrorist outfit. Figure we should look into it, Mr. Wallburg?''

"Yes,'' Katz confirmed. "We also need to find out more about the counterprotesters who charged into the demonstration when Finley and Lincoln were abducted. They certainly served as a good distraction while the kidnapping took place.''

"Perfect timing," McCarter added. "Who were those chaps anyway? I noticed most of them were black and they certainly objected to Finley and Lincoln."

Van Schooer nodded. "Most of those protesters were auto workers, and workers from the Crown Mines and textile factories. They're especially opposed to disinvestment notions that have been encouraged by Bishop Tutu as well as Reverend Jesse Jackson and a number of other so-called do-gooders in the United States."

"Black Africans are paid very well to work in the mines," Sergeant Muspula announced. "Especially the workers at the gold mines. They can afford to support their families and put their children through school—which means better education and more opportunities for blacks in the future. That's why most of us black South Africans don't approve of disinvestment. Tutu wants us to cut our own throats."

"I don't know about that, Sergeant," James began. "But I can't see how it's supposed to help the black population in South Africa if your economy gets in worse shape."

"My God," Muspula said with a grin. "We *almost* agree on something."

"I think we can all agree to check out the counterdemonstrators and find out why they chose that precise moment to interrupt the rally," McCarter stated.

"Good point," Gary Manning agreed. "Another point is the fact the kidnappers escaped in a military Hippo. That suggests that whoever did it were probably disguised as soldiers."

"Quite right," Captain Whitney confirmed. "Two white men were seen herding Finley and Lincoln into the vehicle. No one was alarmed by this, since it was the accepted plan to protect our VIP speakers from injury if any sort of violence occurred. No one got a good look at the blokes, so we don't have a decent description. The driver of the vehicle was a large black man, probably a Zulu."

"Don't rub it in," Muspula said with a snort. "Most of the black soldiers and police are Zulu. We have a very long and proud history as fighting men, you know."

"Two of the kidnappers were white and a third was a black man," Gary Manning mused. "Does that eliminate any suspects from our list?"

"I'm afraid not," van Schooer replied. "There are whites associated with the antiapartheid movement, including the UDF and the FASA. If the Communists are responsible, they may have imported some East Europeans for the job. Perhaps Czechs or East Germans."

"Or Bulgarians," Manning remarked.

"If the enemy is a white-militant group, they may have hired some black hoodlums for their scheme," Karl Hahn added. "Which leaves us right where we started."

"We haven't really started yet," Katz corrected, "and it's about time we do."

6

The Toyota Corolla cruised down Bree Street toward the Fordsburg section of Johannesburg. Sergeant Muspula was once again at the steering wheel. Calvin James and Gary Manning sat in the back of the sturdy Japanese car.

"Tell me, Sergeant," James began, "now that we're not around van Schooer and Whitney, are you really as gung ho on the South African government as you seemed to be back there?"

"Gung ho?" Muspula chuckled. "Do you mean am I in favor of apartheid? I'm a black man. Of course I don't like being a second-class citizen in my own country."

"So you were just paying lip service to the government?" Manning inquired.

"Not at all," Muspula corrected. "The government doesn't grant equality to blacks or coloreds, but things are still better for us than they were twenty years ago. Isn't that the way it was in America? Blacks slowly got more rights until you achieved equality?"

"But don't you get impatient waiting for change?" James asked.

"This is Africa," the sergeant stated. "Change comes slowly, except for changes through violent revolution. Those can be very quick and very bad. Amin came to power that way. And Obote. And the Communists are also trying to claim Africa, bit by bit. Here in South Africa we have people who have come to our country to live from virtually every other nation in the continent. Do you know why? Because blacks have more freedom here than they do in any of the other countries. There is no starvation in South Africa. Even our poor are better off than most who live in Zaire or Uganda."

"Maybe," James allowed. "But you're not equals here. Racial discrimination is national policy. You can't own a home in a white neighborhood. The income for whites is five times higher than it is for blacks."

"That's true," Muspula agreed. "But things are changing and if they change too quickly it can be a disaster. Look at what happened in Rhodesia. The United States, Great Britain, the U.N., all urged rapid change in Rhodesia. Eventually, the whites in power were removed. Robert Mugabe and Joshua Nkomo took over. They were the leaders of the Patriotic Front, a guerrilla army that had fought against Prime Minister Ian Smith for many years. Most of the victims of the Patriotic Front were *black* Rhodesians. Women were raped, villages burned to the ground, men tortured to death. A favorite tactic of these terrorists was to cut off the lips and ears of their victims as a warning to others not to support Smith's government."

"I remember seeing photographs of alleged victims," Manning commented.

"Alleged?" Muspula laughed. "There was nothing 'alleged' about it. Even your American media, which was always critical of Smith's regime, eventually had to admit such atrocities were taking place in Rhodesia. The terrorists were armed with AK-47 assault rifles and addressed each other as 'comrade.' Their main bases were in Angola, supervised by Cubans who were likewise supervised by the Soviets. It shouldn't surprise anyone that Zimbabwe is a hellhole far worse than anything Rhodesia had been in the past."

"Haven't really heard too much about Zimbabwe since Mugabe took over," James confessed.

"Your American media doesn't care if blacks kill blacks," Muspula stated. "That's what's been happening in Zimbabwe. Mugabe and Nkomo became rivals. They've been fighting each other ever since. A bloodbath has been taking place in Zimbabwe, but the Americans, the English and the U.N. choose to look the other way. Perhaps they don't wish to acknowledge what sort of government they helped put into power. Many tourists in Zimbabwe have been kidnapped and murdered. The standard of living, industrialization, medical care and production of foreign exports have dropped drastically. Mugabe has cut social programs, raised taxes and pretty well driven the economy into the ground. We South Africans, black as well as white, have no desire to see the same thing happen to our country."

"Even if you have to tolerate apartheid?" James asked.

"As long as the changes continue to happen," Muspula confirmed. "And those changes remain *positive*."

At last, they arrived at their destination. The headquarters of the Free All South Africans group was a large three-story house with iron bars in the windows. Two young black men stood on the porch, watching the Corolla with suspicion as Muspula applied the brakes and parked the car. The three men opened the doors and stepped from the vehicle.

"Nyumba-kosefu, n'guruwe," one of the youths on the porch declared gruffly.

"What did he say?" Gary Manning asked Muspula.

"Don't ask me," the sergeant replied. "I don't speak Swahili."

"I told you this is the wrong house," the youth said sharply. "And I called you a pig."

"Aren't we off to a friendly start?" Muspula said to his companions.

"Look, kid," Calvin James said, "I'm an American. We didn't come here to hassle you dudes. Just got some questions to ask."

"You're an American?" The young man seemed interested. "Does this concern the kidnapping? Are you a journalist?"

"Who is the white man with you?" the other youth demanded.

"I'm his press secretary," Gary Manning replied. "We didn't come here to play Twenty Questions with you guys. Will you just tell whoever is in charge we want to talk to him?"

"I am in charge," a voice announced from the open door of the building. "I will talk to you, American."

The young men stepped aside as a middle-aged black man stepped from the threshold. His iron-gray hair was clipped close to his skull, and a black patch covered his right eye. He limped as he shuffled across the porch, leaning heavily on a thick wooden cane.

"My name is Cromo," he announced. "Phillip Cromo, district chairman of the Free All South Africans."

"District Chairman?" Muspula raised his eyebrows. "I didn't think your organization was large enough to need more than one chairman."

"We're larger than you realize," Cromo declared. "You've been licking the boots of the Afrikaners so much, you haven't had time to see what is happening around you."

"And whose boots have you been tasting, Cromo?" Muspula sneered. "Cuban or Russian?"

"You've been listening to too much propaganda," Cromo said with a shrug.

"The Soviets are running entire countries throughout Africa," Muspula replied. "That's not just propaganda."

"Shut up about politics," James snapped. "We don't have all day. Two Americans were kidnapped, Mr. Cromo. You know anything about it?"

"You're not journalists?" the FASA leader inquired.

"No," James replied, "so don't bother giving us a speech about peace and freedom."

"Oh." Cromo smiled thinly. "I think it's too late for peace. Peaceful protests haven't gotten us much results in the past. The time is coming when blacks and coloreds will have to stand up and demand equality. If the white supremacists deny us, we'll simply have to claim freedom by force."

"Sounds like you don't mind if a lot of people get killed in the process," Manning commented.

"What do you know about South Africa?" Cromo demanded. He hobbled down the steps, glaring at the Canadian with his single eye. "Twenty years ago, I was a sound, healthy man. Until four drunken white soldiers decided to have some sport by beating up a kaffir. They knocked me to the ground and kicked me like a disobedient dog. They stomped on my leg, breaking bones in three places. One of them kicked me in the face and the eyeball burst in its socket."

Cromo shook with anger as he continued. "And what punishment did the whites receive for crippling and half-blinding me? They were fined. Each of them had to pay fifty rand for what they did to me! Two hundred rand for maiming a kaffir. I spent three months flat on my back in a segregated hospital where I received inferior medical care."

"A lot has changed in twenty years," Muspula declared.

"It has?" Cromo laughed bitterly. "I still must show proper identification to the police if they stop me in the street. I must carry a passport as if I am a foreigner in my own country. The government can still ban me from neighborhoods or cities, or order me to stay at home. I can be denied freedom of speech. None of this has changed."

"Okay," James began, "I'm convinced the South African government shouldn't win any humanitarian awards from the NAACP. But I'm not convinced they kidnapped Senator Finley and Reverend Lincoln, either."

"You don't think *we* did it?" Cromo seemed startled. "Those men were our allies. They came to speak for our cause. They came to help us...."

"And get some publicity for themselves," James declared. "I got some bad news for you, man. Politicians are pretty much the same everywhere in the world. They're all concerned with publicity, pleasing special-interest groups and getting reelected. Those guys knew if they made a trip to South Africa to protest apartheid they'd get coverage on prime-time TV. That's more important to most of those dudes in public office than any human rights issue.''

"Are all Americans so cynical?" Cromo snorted.

"Several politicians have been arrested protesting at the South African embassy in America," James stated. "Some have come here to protest in your country. None of them have made such sacrifices to protest the genocide in Cambodia. None of them have traveled to Southeast Asia to protest the murders of over three million people that have taken place there since the Americans pulled out of Vietnam. There hasn't been much said about it, period.''

"What's your point?" Cromo demanded.

"We've got about twenty-five million black voters in the United States and only a handful of Southeast Asians registered to vote," James explained. "I figure that has something to do with why politicians find South Africa to be a more popular target than Cambodia. I figure you FASA folks are bright enough to realize the same thing.''

"Reverend Lincoln is not a politician...." Cromo began.

"Every major religious leader is part politician," Gary Manning stated. "Jerry Falwell, Reverend Moon or the Pope, they're all involved in politics as well as religion. Hell, Jesse Jackson ran for President. If that's not politics, what is?''

"And they all love headlines," James added. "So do most political action groups. Seems to me FASA wouldn't have too much trouble rationalizing how a couple of gloryhound Americans could be more valuable as martyrs to your cause than part-time supporters in the U.S.''

"After all," Manning commented, "if another popular cause comes along, those fellas will drop the apartheid issue like a hot potato.''

"Your accusations are absurd," Cromo snapped. "We're freedom fighters, not terrorists. Why don't you harass the gangsters who run South Africa? They kidnapped Finley and Lincoln to shut them up.''

"Shit." James shook his head. "The government wouldn't have allowed them to enter the country in the first place if that was true. We're looking into the possibility somebody within the government might be responsible, but you dudes aren't above suspicion, either. How about a little cooperation?"

"Cooperate?" Cromo laughed bitterly. "I can't help you with something I know nothing about. FASA is nonviolent and none of us would ever agree to kidnapping or bloodshed."

"Is that why you've been storing weapons and ammunition?" Sergeant Muspula inquired. "Don't bother denying this, Cromo. The BSS knows that your group has been buying guns from black-market sources and from the Communists in Angola."

"Do you want to search our headquarters?" the FASA leader invited. "You won't even find a slingshot, Sergeant."

"We don't know where your cache of arms is hidden," Muspula confessed, "but we know you've got weapons and explosives. Sooner or later we'll find them and that's when you'll go to jail."

"*If* we have a cache of weapons," Cromo began, "and I'm not saying we do, it would be kept for defensive purposes in case you and your white masters attack us."

"You've already admitted you'd be willing to resort to a violent revolution," Muspula reminded him.

"As a last resort," the FASA boss said with a nod. "Until we've reached our limit, the protests against apartheid will continue to be nonviolent."

"Like the protesters last year who murdered four or five black Americans for not joining their cause?" Manning asked dryly.

"Do you know how many times the police and the military have shot demonstrators?" Cromo replied angrily. "A certain amount of retribution was bound to occur."

"Quit fuckin' around with us," Calvin James said sharply. "Not all your followers are nonviolent. You've obviously got some hotheads among the FASA and probably the United Democratic Front, as well. Don't tell me none of your people would kidnap two American VIPs if they thought it might get the South African government in hot water."

"What about the hotheads in government?" Cromo demanded.

"We're trying that angle too," Manning assured him. "Now, are you going to check within your organization and see if you have any extremists who might have kidnapped Finley and Lincoln?"

"I don't intend to give you people an easy scapegoat," Cromo answered.

"Cromo," James began, "let me tell you something about the group I work with. We get results. Sometimes we shit all over people's rights and sometimes we kill them, but we always get results. If you're holding out on us, we'll find out. We specialize in kicking the shit out of bad guys."

"And who are the bad guys?" Cromo asked stiffly.

"In this case," James replied, "whoever kidnapped Finley and Lincoln. We don't care if the guilty parties turn out to be black, white or polka-dotted, man. When we find who did it, we'll stomp them into the ground."

"Please understand, Mr. Cromo," Manning added quickly. "We're not hired killers and we don't murder people in cold blood, but most of our enemies don't live to stand trial. They usually put up a fight. In combat we believe in the law of the jungle: kill or be killed."

"Are you threatening me?" Cromo asked, trying to decide if these two Americans were really as tough as they seemed.

"Not at all," James assured him. "If your group isn't involved in the kidnapping, you've got nothing to worry about from us. But you'd better make certain none of your FASA pals are moonlighting as abductors."

"Actually," Manning went on, "if Finley and Lincoln were released, pretty much in one piece, we'd be perfectly happy to take them back to the States and let you South Africans quarrel with each other about who's at fault. We'd rather do this the easy way, but we're used to doing things the hard way. And we are very good at our job."

"What if Finley and Lincoln are already dead?" Cromo asked, a tremor in his voice.

"Then we'll find out who killed them," James said with a shrug. "And we'll bring them to justice. Probably through the barrel of a gun."

"I'll talk to my people," Cromo said grimly. "But I want your word that you'll continue to investigate members of the white establishment as well."

"You've got it," James assured him.

"If that concludes our discussion," Cromo began, "I believe I'll get out of the sun. May I give you two a word of advice?"

"Can't promise we'll take it," Manning answered.

"Be careful how hard you push people." Cromo smiled thinly. "That can be very dangerous in South Africa."

7

"Do you believe Cromo?" Sergeant Muspula inquired as he drove the Corolla away from the FASA headquarters.

"I don't know," Calvin James replied to the BSS sergeant beside him. "I'm inclined to believe Cromo doesn't know anything about the kidnapping, but I don't think he's really as sure about the others in his group as he claims to be."

"Cromo is certainly a bitter man," Gary Manning added. "But I guess you can't blame him for having a chip on his shoulder after what he's been through."

"He's dangerous," Muspula insisted. "One of these days, we'll have to clean out that rat pack at the FASA head shed."

"Well, that's..." James began. His sentence ended abruptly when he noticed a blue car was moving up behind them. Red lights on its roof flashed as the vehicle drew closer.

"Police," Muspula commented calmly. "Probably a routine stop."

"Routine?" Manning frowned. "They stop you very often?"

"They stop blacks all the time," Muspula said, sighing. "Too bad we didn't have a staff car. They'd probably leave us alone then."

The sergeant pulled over to the curb and parked. The police car rolled to a stop right behind the Corolla. Muspula donned his uniform cap and opened the door. He unbuttoned his khaki shirt to get out his ID.

"You'd better get your passports ready, too," he advised. "Especially you, Mr. Walker."

"What?" James replied. He had almost forgotten his cover name. "Yeah. Better keep the Man happy."

As Muspula stepped from the car, Manning glanced over his shoulder to peer out the rear window. Two white men dressed in blue uniforms had emerged from the cop car. One officer carried an Israeli Uzi in his fists while the other dragged a Belgium-made NATO 9 mm FN pistol from the holster on his hip. Manning reached inside his linen jacket and grabbed the Pachmayr grips of the Israeli Eagle under his left arm.

"Cal," the Canadian whispered.

"I noticed," James replied softly. "I'm just not sure if this is standard procedure with the cops around here or not."

Suddenly, the cop with the pistol raised his weapon and opened fire. Muspula cried out as the officer pumped two 9 mm Parabellum rounds into the sergeant's chest. Muspula toppled to the ground, his tunic splashed with blood. The cop with the Uzi trained his subgun on the Corolla.

James and Manning instantly dropped to the floorboards as the Uzi slashed a stream of 9 mm slugs into the vehicle. Fragments of shattered glass showered down on the Phoenix Force pair. Manning clenched his teeth as a shard of glass bit into the exposed flesh at the back of his neck. The Canadian's highly disciplined mind reacted to the unexpected attack with computer efficiency and the split-second speed born of desperation.

They had two options. Remain boxed up in the car and allow the two gunmen to close in on either side and blast them with a deadly cross fire, or try to bolt from the vehicle and shoot back. The former meant certain death and the chances of survival from the latter were slim. Lousy odds beats no odds, the Canadian decided as he jerked down the handle and shoved the door open.

Gary Manning threw himself from the car, turning slightly to land on his side. Both hands fisted around the Eagle pistol as he pointed the big autoloader at the nearest opponent. As the cop with the handgun swung his weapon toward Manning, the Phoenix fighter triggered the Eagle. The big Magnum pistol roared and bucked sharply in Manning's grasp.

A .357 Glasier Safety slug crashed into the policeman's chest. Designed to spend full energy on a target on impact, the slug expanded when it struck, blasting the gunman's sternum and driving bone shrapnel into his heart and lungs. The cop's body hopped backward and fell heavily to the ground.

The killer with the Uzi quickly aimed his blaster at the Canadian. Calvin James had already emerged from the opposite side of the Corolla, Colt Commander held in a Weaver combat position. He fired the pistol, arms raising slightly with the familiar recoil of the powerful handgun. The killer cop shrieked when the .45-caliber projectile punched into his right shoulder, tearing the deltoid and shattering the joint.

The impact spun the gunsel around. He still held the Uzi, pointing the submachine gun in the general direction of Calvin James. The black warrior did not hesitate. He fired another shot, pumping a 185-grain Silvertip hollowpoint into his opponent's upper torso. The second bullet smashed into the top of the cop's breastbone and sliced an upward tunnel into the gunman's throat. The assassin dropped his weapon and crumpled to the pavement.

"Jesus," Manning rasped. "What the hell's going on?"

"Check on Muspula," James urged as he jogged toward the bodies of the two killer cops.

The Canadian knelt beside Sergeant Muspula and placed two fingers to the inside of the BSS man's wrist. He found no pulse. Manning shook his head sadly as he pressed lightly on Muspula's eyelids to close them.

"The sergeant's dead," Manning told his partner.

"So are these two bastards," James replied, having checked the police officers for signs of life. He was not very disappointed when he failed to find any.

"I'm going to radio home base and tell them what happened," Manning announced as he climbed into the front seat. "We'd better not try to take off until van Schooer and his people give us the green light. Otherwise, we might get in hot water with the *real* Johannesburg police."

"I just hope these dudes *weren't* real cops," James replied gravely.

The black man glanced about at the surrounding street. They had been ambushed in a residential area, but there were no pedestrians on the sidewalks. In the heat of the gun battle, James had not had time to notice the area or whether or not anyone witnessed the incident. Curtains moved at windows, but no one ventured from their homes.

Then James heard the creak of door hinges and turned to see a pair of hard-faced Afrikaners step onto a porch. Both men carried pump-action shotguns.

"Oh, shit," James muttered under his breath. "Looks like we might have some vigilantes in the neighborhood, man!"

"What did you say?" Manning called back, busy with the CB in the car.

"I said we're gonna die, damn it!" Calvin snapped. He carefully placed his Colt Commander on the ground and raised his hands to assure the Afrikaners he offered no threat.

"Whitney and Katz should be arriving any minute," Manning announced as he slipped from the Corolla. The Canadian was surprised to see James holding his arms in the air. "Now what?"

"Get over here, man," James urged. "I think these guys might be a little less eager to use those riot guns if they see your lily-white face."

"Hi," Manning told the Afrikaners as he raised his hands. "I hope you guys noticed we acted in self-defense."

The two shotgunners did not respond. They held their weapons with the barrels pointing down, apparently uncertain if the two men in the street were terrorists or victims. They seemed more concerned about protecting their homes than avenging the slain police officers. Perhaps they had seen the gun battle and realized Manning and James had been forced to shoot the cops. The incident must have seemed very muddled to the civilians.

"I don't think they're going to shoot us," Manning told his partner. "But I wouldn't make any quick movements."

"I wouldn't think of it," James assured the Canadian. He noticed the sun was bisected by the horizon and the sky was slowly growing darker. "Hope we don't have to stand out here all night."

"Yeah," Manning agreed. "Maybe we . . ."

The wail of a siren announced the arrival of another police car. The blue vehicle swung onto the street, red lights flashing and brakes screeching as the car came to an abrupt halt. Doors opened and two cops jumped from the auto, pistols in their fists.

"Just relax, officers," James urged, stepping forward to gesture toward the body of Sergeant Muspula. "Let us explain. . . ."

"Stoppen, kheffur!" one of the policemen snarled, pointing his gun at James.

"That means, 'halt, nigger,'" the other cop stated as he approached the Phoenix Force pair.

"I just love studying linguistics in this country," James muttered sourly.

"Shut your mouth, *zwartie*," the English-speaking cop snapped. He was a large, burly white man who was clearly used to being obeyed by "lesser races" in Johannesburg.

"Turn around and put your hands on the roof of that Toyota. Feet apart. You know how to do this, don't you?"

"I used to be a cop back in America," James assured him as he turned to face the car.

"Nigger cop," the policeman sneered with contempt as he suddenly shoved James. The black man grunted when he fell against the body of the Corolla.

"Hey, fella..." Gary Manning began, but the other cop pushed him into the car as well. The hard muzzle of a pistol jabbed into the small of Manning's spine.

"Nich bewegen, wit kheffur," a voice hissed near Manning's ear.

"Officer Matroos warned you not to move, white nigger," the English-speaking cop explained. "There are two dead police officers on the ground, so we'll be pretty willing to shoot you both if you give us any shit."

"Passport is in my inside pocket," James explained. "Right side of the jacket, man. There's also..."

Without warning, the big cop hammered the butt of his pistol between James's shoulder blades. The Phoenix pro groaned as his body smacked against the car. He gasped for breath, winded by the unexpected blow. The cop jammed his gun into James's ribs as he began to search the black man.

"I already told you to shut up, nigger," the policemen stated. "By the way, my name is Officer Pulver—if you want to try to prosecute me for excessive behavior. Not that anyone will listen to you, black monkey."

James wanted to hit back. He was certain he could disarm Pulver with a whirling elbow stroke, and then he could kick the bigoted cop's ass all over the street. However, James did not resist as the cop groped inside his jacket. Fingers pulled the G-96 Jet Aer dagger from the sheath clipped to the straps of James's shoulder holster under his right arm.

"Carrying a concealed weapon," Pulver remarked as he tossed the knife aside. "And that holster means you were carrying a gun as well."

"I was gonna tell you about the knife before you hit me," James said quickly, wanting to complete the sentence before Pulver could slug him again.

Officer Matroos had found and confiscated Gary Manning's Eagle pistol. The Canadian demolitions expert also carried several pencil-detonators in his shirt pocket and six ounces of C-4 plastic explosives concealed in a money-belt compartment, but the cop failed to find these as he completed his frisk.

"So you and the nigger-lover are both carrying weapons," Pulver remarked. "I think that's reason to arrest you for killing two police officers."

"We've got pistol permits from the BSS," Manning declared. "Look at the sergeant. He's wearing an army uniform. He was from the bureau."

"Just looks like another monkey with clothes on to me." Pulver snickered. "But the two policemen you killed were white."

"They weren't real cops," James told him.

Pulver angrily kicked one of James's ankles. The black man lost his balance and fell at the cop's feet. Pulver slammed a boot into the black warrior's ribs. James gasped and glared up at the policeman's pistol, pointed at his face.

"You son of a bitch," Manning rasped.

Officer Matroos swatted the barrel of his pistol across the back of Manning's skull. The Canadian's chin rapped against the car roof as his head bounced from the blow. Matroos stamped a boot to the back of Manning's knee. The leg buckled and the Phoenix fighter moaned and abruptly fell to his knees. The hard steel cylinder of Matroos's pistol poked behind his ear, daring him to fight back.

"They weren't real cops?" Pulver growled as he stared down at Calvin James. "You think some goddamn nigger could be a real cop, eh?"

Pulver suddenly kicked James in the stomach. The black man convulsed in pain and raised his knees to protect his groin and abdomen. Then Pulver spit on James, his saliva splattering on the black man's sleeve as James shielded his face and head with his arms.

"You Americans make me sick," Pulver said with a sneer. "You don't care if your races mix together. They let niggers like you do whatever they please. No wonder cities in America are jungles of crime and drug abuse when they do not exercise proper control of the conduct of black apes like you."

He kicked James again, his boot striking the SWAT vet's thigh muscle. "And you think you can come to South Africa and kill policemen as if you were still in New York or Chicago?" Pulver snarled. "The hell you will, you stinking savage!"

A large black car suddenly roared up the street. A blinking red light was mounted on the roof, although the vehicle was not labelled as a police car. A door opened and Yakov Katzenelenbogen hopped from the sedan before it came to a full stop.

"Let those men up!" Katz demanded, his eyes as hard as blue flint as he glared at the Johannesburg cops. The Israeli's left hand was inside his jacket, ready to draw his SIG-Sauer automatic if the policemen failed to obey.

"What is this?" Pulver asked, stepping away from Calvin James. "We are simply doing our duty...."

"You bloody idiots!" Captain Whitney shouted as he emerged from the sedan. "These men are working with the BSS on special assignment in the republic."

"How could we have known that?" Pulver inquired with a helpless shrug. "We found two dead police officers so naturally..."

"You decided to conduct a beating in public?" Whitney fumed. "I'm going to see to it you two wind up behind bars with the other criminals. I'm sure you'll get a warm reception when the convicts find out what line of work you blokes were in before you pulled this stupid stunt!"

"You can't blame us," Pulver insisted. "We didn't know who they were."

"We told you, damn it!" Manning snapped as he climbed to his feet. "You bastards didn't even look at our passports."

"Wait a moment," Pulver began, returning his pistol to its holster. "You fellows did try to resist us and you were not very co-operative."

"Ist fout, ja?" Matroos said with a smile. "Mistake?"

"A mistake." Katzenelenbogen nodded as he approached the Afrikaner cop. "Well, mistakes do happen."

The Israeli lashed out a boot and kicked Matroos squarely in the balls. The cop doubled up with an agonized gasp, clutching at his genitals with both hands.

"My foot slipped," Katz muttered through clenched teeth. "Another mistake."

His left fist crashed into Matroos's jaw. The cop spun about from the punch and started to fall. Gary Manning caught him, grabbing Matroos by the shirtfront. The Canadian's expression was calm, but his eyes burned with anger. He folded a knee and rammed it between Matroos's legs. The blow to his already-battered testicles sent a volt of white-hot agony throughout the cop's nervous system. Manning swung a solid right cross to Matroos's face. The punch knocked him six feet, and he fell to the ground in an unconscious lump.

"Everybody calm down," Officer Pulver urged, holding his hands up as if fending off invisible forces. "There's no call for this sort of behavior—"

"Take off that gun belt, motherfucker!" a voice rasped.

Pulver turned to see Calvin James had risen to his feet. The black warrior stood in a *T-dachi* fighting stance, his hands poised for battle, fingers arched like claws. Pulver slowly unbuckled his gun belt.

"You're asking for more trouble, nigger," the cop said with a sigh.

"You try to give it to me *now*, asshole," James invited.

Pulver suddenly lashed out with the gun belt, trying to whip the holstered pistol across Calvin's face. The black

Phoenix pro dodged the attack, pivoted sharply and whipped a wheel kick to Pulver's abdomen. The back of James's heel slammed into the cop's gut.

James chopped the side of his hand across Pulver's wrist, striking the belt from his opponent's hand. Then he snapped a backfist to the cop's face, and a knuckle split Pulver's upper lip. The bigot stumbled, but did not fall. James slashed a cross-body karate chop, aimed at Pulver's right temple.

The cop ducked under the black man's arm and drove a fist into James's breadbasket. Calvin grunted and promptly smashed the heel of a palm under his opponent's jaw. Pulver's head snapped back and he staggered into the Corolla. The cop shook his head to clear it and launched himself at James once more.

The Phoenix pro's leg shot out in a high tae kwon-do side kick. His foot crashed into the center of Pulver's face, breaking the cop's nose. The force of the kick knocked Pulver to the ground. Dazed, he still tried to get up. James stomped his opponent, driving a heel into Pulver's abdomen, just above the groin.

Pulver's mouth fell open as he groaned, and James spit in the cop's face, firing saliva into the man's gaping mouth. Pulver rolled on his side and began to vomit. James prepared to launch another kick, but decided his opponent had had enough.

"You're not worth wasting my time on, man," James muttered as he walked away from the vanquished cop.

8

Senator Thomas Finley sat on the dirt floor of the primitive cell. His clothes were dirty and clung to his flesh from sweat. Whisker stubble had begun to grow along his jawline and his own body odor offended his nostrils. Reverend Robert Lincoln sat at the opposite corner of the cell, whispering softly as he prayed.

"Jesus," Finley said hoarsely, wiping the back of a hand across his sweat-soaked brow. "Is that all you're going to do? Sit there and pray all day?"

"Maybe it's what I should have been doing before this happened," Lincoln replied with a sigh. "Besides, what do you suggest we do instead?"

Finley glanced about at the gray stone walls that surrounded them. The cell appeared to be part of a cave, a natural fortress of solid granite. Iron bars had been added to block off the cell from the rest of the cave. An armed guard was stationed at the door, a black African who did not seem to understand a single word of English. He totally ignored the Americans' efforts to communicate as he sat in a chair behind his field desk, leafing through magazines by candlelight and sipping cold tea.

Escape seemed impossible. The kidnappers had taken everything from Finley and Lincoln except shirts, trousers and underwear. They had even confiscated the reverend's gold cross. Finley doubted they could have dug their way through solid rock with anything less than power-drilling tools anyway. The bars seemed very solid and the guard never strayed from his post. The bastard even relieved himself at his station, urinating into a tin bucket kept under his desk. The guard never got close enough to the bars for the captives to attempt to overpower him. This seemed rather pointless anyway, since the sentry did not have the key to their cell.

Of course, the guard did have a gun. Neither Finley nor Lincoln had ever been in the armed forces, and neither knew anything about guns except which end to hold. Even if they could get the pistol from the guard and manage to shoot the lock off the cell door, there were other villains beyond the cave and all of them had guns and knew how to use them.

"We can try to negotiate with their leader," Finley decided. "We're skilled public speakers, Robert. I'm sure we can talk our way out of this mess if we can just meet with the leader."

"Maybe the leader doesn't speak English," Reverend Lincoln replied wearily.

"The two jokers who shoved us into the van that brought us here spoke English," Finley reminded the reverend.

"So what?" Lincoln said with a shrug. "Those two were just dumb flunkies. Look, Tom. All we can do is pray that God will deliver us from this evil."

"I never heard you talk like this before." Finley frowned.

"I've never been a prisoner held by a bunch of cutthroats before," Lincoln answered. "Oh, I've been arrested for political protests back in the States. But I was always out on bail before the news appeared on TV. These guys aren't interested in our status and they don't give a shit about our rights, Tom. It'll take a miracle for us to get out of here. That's what I'm praying for."

"Somebody will find us," Finley insisted. "Maybe the CIA or somebody. They're probably planning how to rescue us right now."

"I wouldn't count on that," Lincoln said. "What do you think would happen if somebody does try to rescue us?

They'll probably kill us right here in this cell before they agree to release us.''

"We can't give up hope," Finley insisted.

"There is always hope," Lincoln agreed. "Hope for the Lord's salvation. You know, I've been a pretty sorry excuse for a man of the cloth. I've spent too much time with politics. Too much time being a celebrity. I've been talking about the oppressed in order to appear on more TV programs and talk shows. I didn't go into the ministry to become a star. I never realized until now how far I've drifted from the path of Jesus. If He were to come into His father's house and found me at the pulpit, I would have been driven out with the rest of the merchants."

"Do me a favor and shut up," Finley said sourly.

"*Pua!*" a voice called from the mouth of the cave.

"*Bunduki!*" the sentry cried back in reply.

"*Fanya tenah,*" the voice demanded.

"*Bunduki,*" the guard repeated. "*Ja, rafiki.*"

"*Kivulana-ema.*" Goodman, the Alabama gunman who had helped kidnap Lincoln and Finley, spoke as he approached the guard. "You're a good nigger, aren't you?"

"*N'ido, rafiki.*" The guard smiled and nodded in reply.

"Howdy, boys," Goodman greeted Finley and Lincoln. He carried two small tin pails in his fist. "Reckon you wonder what all that gobbledygook was all about."

"I couldn't understand a word either of you said," Finley admitted.

"Didn't figure you boys spoke no Swahili," Goodman said with a chuckle. "Just speak a little of it myself. See, we was talkin' passwords to each other. If I said the wrong password to the nigger here, then he would have shot both of you dead as a doornail. If he didn't answer the passwords right, then I would've tossed a couple of grenades in with you boys and killed the lot of you. You'd best hope none of us gets a loss of memory, huh?"

"I want to speak to your leader, Mr. Goodman," Finley declared.

"Who gives a shit what you want, yankee?" Goodman laughed. "Besides, I ain't Western Union, boy. Deliverin' messages ain't part of my job. You're lucky I agreed to bring you this here food."

"At least tell us why we're being held prisoner," Finley pleaded.

"All I know is you boys are supposed to be worth a lot of money," Goodman stated. "And that's all that matters to me. Now, you stand clear of the door and I'll put the slop in the cell so y'all can eat it."

"Slop is right," Senator Finley commented. "The garbage you're feeding us is terrible. Who is responsible for this inhumane treatment? I demand some answers!"

"You don't demand nothin' of me, fat boy," Goodman growled, reaching for the Government Issue Colt 1911-A1 on his hip. "I'd just as soon blow your fuckin' head off as look at you."

"Take it easy, Sergeant," a cultured British voice urged. "No need to let the prisoners upset you so. Simply give them their food and leave."

The voice belonged to a tall man dressed in neatly pressed khaki uniform and a bush hat with a battered brim. He was a white man, roughly forty years old. A rust-colored mustache curled along his upper lip, the ends stiff with wax. He saluted the prisoners by touching the silver head of a swagger stick to the brim of his headgear.

"Good evening, gentlemen," the Briton announced. "Sorry about the conditions, but this business wasn't my idea, you know. I'm just a soldier, commanding other soldiers. The chaps who pay us make the rules. Chain of command and all that."

"Who are you?" Finley asked. "Who are you working for?"

"You can call me Major Kingston," the Briton answered. "I'm the unit commander of a private army of sorts. Of course you know Sergeant Goodman, and I believe you met Sergeant Gruber, as well. Now, the chaps you'll meet here aren't all part of my mercenary group. Most of my blokes are Europeans or British with a couple of Americans thrown in. The only blacks in our unit are a pair of ex-paratroopers from Zaire. Not bad fellows, really. However, I suggest you watch yourself around these Africans. Most of them are Congolese. Nasty buggers and very anti-American. Lot of Marxist influence in the Congo these days."

"You're not anti-American?" Reverend Lincoln inquired as he rose to his feet.

"I'm not antianything," Kingston said with a shrug. "I'm simply a mercenary. No politics, no morals, no lofty causes. I'm interested in money. Frankly, if that means I have to kill you, I'll do it without batting an eye. Nothing personal, you understand. Just the nature of my business."

"And it's your business to kidnap us and hold us captive for your employer?" Finley frowned. "Just for money?"

"It makes the world go round, old boy," Kingston replied.

"If you'll help us escape," Finley began hopefully, "we'll pay you twice, three times what your employer is paying."

"Generous offer," Kingston said with a laugh. "However, I really don't think I could trust you fellows to pay us. After all, we helped abduct you in the first place. How would payment be arranged? Through the mail? By messenger? I have a feeling you'd rather see us behind bars than pay us a small fortune to free you."

"You have my word...." Finley began.

"The word of a politician is probably the most worthless commodity on the face of the earth," the mercenary stated. "You're all liars without any trace of a code of honor."

"You kill people for a living and you criticize our sense of honor?" Reverend Lincoln demanded.

"So you consider yourself a politician, eh, Reverend?" Kingston smiled. "That's interesting. Actually, I have a very strong code of honor, though it is based more on practical economics than principles of morality."

"Let me talk to your boss, damn it," Finley told him. "Get him in here."

"You pompous bastard!" Kingston laughed. "You're in no position to give orders to anyone. My employer will see you when he's damn good and ready and not before. You think because you're a United States senator that means you're important? Right now, you're valuable alive. When that time runs out you'll probably be terminated like an obsolete wall clock. You, Reverend. Do you think your clerical collar means anything to this lot? There's not a Christian among us. Most of these chaps are atheists and the rest are members of old primitive African religions and a couple of fanatic Moslems. None of whom will show you any sort of consideration because you're a minister."

"You'll be lucky if'n they don't skin you alive, boy," Goodman said with a cruel smile.

"My advice to you both is to regard yourselves as prisoners at a place like Alcatraz used to be," Kingston told the captives. "At Alcatraz they gave the inmates food, water, shelter and medical care if needed. Everything else was considered a privilege that had to be earned."

"And how do we earn privileges here?" Lincoln asked.

"I'm sure they'll let you know when the time comes," Kingston replied. "Lovely conversation, but I must be off. I hope we'll have a chance to chat again, gentlemen."

When Major Kingston and Sergeant Goodman had left the cave, Lincoln and Finley examined the two pails Goodman had brought them. One was full of water and the other was a collection of partially chewed food—meat, vegetables, fruit and something similar to oatmeal. The keepers were feeding them leftovers, like a farmer slops his hogs.

Hours dragged by. Another guard replaced the man who had been posted by the cell. He too spoke no English and paid little attention to the captives. The cell was muggy and the air was putrid and stale. Finley and Lincoln were exhausted, but it was difficult to breathe in the stuffy little cell, and they could only lie down on the hard earth floor. Yet eventually, both men drifted into a rather restless slumber.

"Wake up, you swine!" a voice snarled.

Foul-smelling amber liquid splashed over the two captives. They awoke abruptly, repulsed by the stench of the urine that soaked their bodies. Someone had tossed the contents of the guard's latrine on the pair.

They opened their eyes to discover the cell was brilliantly lit up by a two-hundred candlepower, battery-operated lantern. They shielded their eyes with their hands, barely able to see the two figures who stood beyond the bars of their cage.

Both visitors were black. The man who held the lantern was enormous. Over six and a half feet tall, he was thickly built at the shoulders and chest although his waist was narrow. His companion was more than a foot shorter, and his body was round and fat. The lenses of his horn-rimmed glasses flashed as he shook his head.

"Stand up!" the fat man shouted. "Don't they teach you scum manners in the United States?"

Finley and Lincoln slowly got to their feet, squinting as the light continued to burn at their eyes. One of their tormentors chuckled with amusement. The lamp was moved slightly so the light was not trained directly on their faces.

"I am Tai Skrubu," the fat man announced. "You may have heard of me, although I doubt that your memories are good enough to remember my name, or even the name of the country I ruled for the brief period of two and a half months."

"Skrubu?" Reverend Lincoln began. "Your name is familiar—your country's name meant 'staircase' in Swahili."

"Mardaraja," Skrubu confirmed.

"I remember," Lincoln assured him. "Blacks in America were very impressed by you. We regarded your country as a great stride forward for black people throughout the world. Many of us protested when you were removed from power, Mr. President. I was one of your supporters at the time. I thought the British should have been reprimanded for that business at the embassy...."

"Of course," Finley added. "The Mardarajan embassy in London! I remember that too."

"Very good." Skrubu snickered. "You can remember a major news story from last year. Isn't that impressive? As you might recall, the situation in London was similar to the Libyan embassy incident that had occurred some months earlier. Some Britons were shot and killed by snipers, and Mardaraja severed diplomatic relations with England. Of course, we were protected by diplomatic immunity, just as the Libyans had been. My people should have left the embassy and returned to Mardaraja safely, but five mysterious invaders attacked the embassy. Five professional killers who were very good at their job. They slaughtered everyone inside the building with the exception of the coward who was my so-called ambassador."

"He claimed there were Libyan terrorists in the embassy and that Mardaraja was just a puppet power for Libya's Colonel Khaddafi," Lincoln recalled. "I never believed those stories, Mr. President. I figured the British made Ambassador Mufuta say those things."

"Then you're a bigger idiot than I thought you were," replied Skrubu. "Of course, there were Libyans in the embassy and Mardaraja was really run by Khaddafi. That Libyan son of a whore cut off support to my regime after that disaster in London. Two weeks later, an organized revolt began and I was forced to flee the country. Of course, I emptied out the treasury first. I needed money and I still do."

"We can get you money," Finley assured him. "My family is rich. They can probably raise eight, maybe ten million dollars for my release."

"Ten million dollars?" Skrubu laughed bitterly. "I plan to get at least five times that much, you moron. You two are simply pawns in a game I'm playing. Part of a greater plan that will set the stage for the greatest auction of all time. An auction that will make me a very wealthy man.''

"I don't understand," Finley confessed.

"You don't have to understand, white man," Skrubu told him. "All you need to know is I can make your life absolutely hell if you don't cooperate with me. Obey me and you'll be given decent food, clean quarters and clothes. You'll be allowed to bathe and breathe fresh air again. Disobey me and you'll think the treatment you've received so far was wonderful compared to what we'll do to you. Starvation, torture, executions—these are common practices in African politics. Don't think I'd hesitate to use such tactics if you displease me."

Skrubu turned from the cell and headed toward the exit, followed by his huge companion. He stopped and glanced over his shoulder at the cell. "I'm going to let you spend the rest of the night lying on the ground, covered with piss and shivering with fear," he announced. "Come sunup, I'll consider whether or not to allow you to take a bath in water that hasn't already passed through someone else's bladder. Sleep well, gentlemen."

With that, Skrubu departed. Finley and Lincoln sat in the stuffy, dank cell, dripping with urine. The nightmare was getting worse, but both men realized the ultimate horror still waited to become reality.

9

Karl Hahn's fingers danced across the keyboard of the computer terminal. Data appeared across the green viewing screen. The West German agent ran a finger under a line that described a report to the Johannesburg police about a police car that had been stolen the day before.

"This is from the police morning report," Hahn told the other members of Phoenix Force. "The license number matches that of the vehicle that followed Walker and Summer and ambushed them on the street. Apparently, those guys who attacked you were not police officers. Unless, of course, some cops stole the car from their own department."

"Any identification on the dead men?" Katz inquired.

"Photographs of the deceased have been checked and cross-checked," Hahn answered, "but so far neither man has been identified. Interpol might have something on them. One thing is certain, neither of those men were ever members of the Johannesburg police or any other South African law-enforcement agency. In fact, there's a very good chance neither man was a citizen of the republic or even legally in the country."

"They were working for FASA," Pieter van Schooer declared. "I think that's obvious."

"I'm not convinced of that," Gary Manning told the Afrikaner. "After all, FASA didn't attack us when we were at their headquarters."

"No," van Schooer agreed. "They wanted to make it appear that the Johannesburg police were guilty."

"That doesn't make much sense," Calvin James replied. "Phillip Cromo knew Sergeant Muspula was with us. He knew Muspula was BSS. From what we told him, I'm sure that dude realized Summers and I are some sort of covert operatives from America. I don't see why an antiapartheid group would figure a news story about Johannesburg cops gunning down a government agent and two American snoops would spark any sympathy for their cause. Hell, it doesn't even make sense."

"A lot of what the antiapartheid groups do doesn't make much sense," the Afrikaner remarked.

"Hey, man," James said sharply. "Don't get me started on the apartheid policies in this country. Not after what happened with those cops today. And I mean the real cops."

"I'm sorry about what happened to you and Mr. Summers," van Schooer said. "But you can't blame all of us for what two unpleasant police officers did to you."

"I wouldn't describe those jerks as 'unpleasant,'" Manning commented dryly. "Pistol-whipping is a little more than rudeness."

"I'm not defending what those policemen did," the Afrikaner assured him. "Yet incidents of police brutality occur everywhere. Don't tell me such things are unheard of in the United States."

"Well," James said, "at least we got to kick the shit out of those two creeps. Our real concern is who sent those phony cops to try to waste us."

"It must have been the Communists," Captain Whitney remarked as he slumped into a chair near Hahn's desk. "Whether you want to hear this or not, Mr. Walker, the agents of Moscow are involved with the antiapartheid movement. The men who tried to kill you were probably East European assassins."

"We have to consider that possibility," Katz agreed, shaking a cigarette from a pack of Camels. "But we can't disregard other possibilities. Anybody could hire outside hit men. Just because the gunmen weren't South Africans doesn't prove they were working for the Soviets."

"We can't be certain the killers weren't South Africans," Hahn reminded him. "Just because there hasn't been any identification by computer check doesn't prove those fellows were outsiders. We don't have enough facts to draw any conclusions."

David McCarter entered the safe house, accompanied by a tall black man. The Briton's companion wore a South African army uniform with the insignia of sergeant major on his sleeve. He smiled at the men of Phoenix Force, revealing teeth that sparkled as brightly as the diamond pin clipped to the corner of his right nostril.

"Hello, mates," McCarter greeted. "I hear you had a bit of excitement. Wish we could say the same."

"If we hadn't found a pleasant tavern on the way back to the city," the black sergeant major added, "it would have been a total waste of time."

"You blokes haven't met Sergeant Major Oktoba yet," the Briton explained. "The sergeant was part of the security unit protecting Finley and Lincoln."

"I hate to admit this," Oktoba said, "but I personally shoved the senator off the platform to the 'safety' of the Hippo. It seemed like the right thing to do at the time."

"No one suspected a kidnapping attempt until after it happened," Katz assured him. "I take it you didn't find any useful information by talking to the workers at the Crown Mines?"

"Only a few of the miners were part of the counterdemonstration that protested at the rally for Finley and Lincoln," McCarter answered. "They joined the demonstration because they object to disinvestment. They figure if Americans stop buying Krugerands, the demand for gold will drop and jobs for gold miners will suffer."

"Do they know who organized the counterdemonstration?" Karl Hahn inquired.

"Apparently it was put together by the leader of one of the textile unions," McCarter explained. "However, plans for the protest weren't exactly a state secret. The newspapers had run a story on it, and it was common knowledge for at least a week before Finley and Lincoln arrived. There was a similar demonstration during a speech Senator Kennedy made when he was in South Africa last year. That incident didn't turn into a riot, so the authorities didn't expect the situation to get nasty."

"So virtually anyone could have known about the demonstration and planned to use it for a distraction in order to abduct Lincoln and Finley," Katz commented.

"What about the riot?" Manning inquired. "They couldn't be certain that would happen."

"It's bloody easy to start a riot when you've got two groups of blokes who violently disagree on an issue to begin with," McCarter replied. "All you need is a couple of chaps in the crowd to throw a few punches and everybody else will start swinging. So simple *anybody* could have arranged it. Which puts us back to square one, unless you people came up with something new."

"Well," James said, "somebody tried to kill us, so we must be closer to uncovering something than any of us suspect."

"It has to be the FASA," van Schooer insisted. "After all, you were attacked after you met with Cromo and his lot."

"That's correct," Karl Hahn said thoughtfully. "Muspula was driving an unmarked car away from the FASA headquarters building, right?"

"Yeah," James agreed. "So maybe the killers thought we were members of FASA and that's why they attacked us."

"Seems like a logical possibility," Hahn said, nodding.

"Good Lord!" van Schooer exclaimed. "You men are trying to invent some sort of excuse to avoid accusing the antiapartheid forces."

"I think you chaps are grasping for straws a bit," Captain Whitney agreed. "The men who were tailing you must have known Sergeant Muspula was in the military, even if they didn't realize he was BSS. One look at his cap would tell them as much."

"Muspula wasn't wearing his cap," Manning declared. "I remember, he put his hat on after he stopped the car and started to get out."

"Even if that's true . . ." van Schooer began.

"Was ist das?" Hahn remarked, raising his eyebrows with interest when he noticed a message on the screen of his computer. "Just got a police report from the link to the Pretoria security computers."

"What is it, Mr. Kruger?" Katz asked, referring to Hahn by his cover name.

"Not good news," the German agent replied. "Two police officers were killed in Pretoria at 2030 hours approximate. About half an hour ago. Someone blew them to pieces with a pipe bomb. Standard terrorist tactics."

"Ja." Van Schooer nodded. "And it is clear what sort of terrorists did this. You gentlemen wanted evidence. Now we have it. FASA or the United Democratic Front must be responsible. Probably both organizations, in league with the Communists, are involved in this conspiracy."

"Wait a minute," Katz said sharply. "We don't even know the two incidents are related."

"Two attacks on law-enforcement personnel in less than four hours and you don't think there's a connection?" Van Schooer glared at the Israeli. "It's obvious you can discard the theory that the killers thought Muspula and your men were FASA members. There's no longer any doubt who the enemy have set their sights on."

"The time element *does* suggest a connection," Karl Hahn announced. "But it is still possible the theory about the attack on Muspula and my friends might be accurate. If you'll give me a moment, I'll explain why."

"Very well, Mr. Kruger," the Afrikaner said with a sigh.

"Danke," Hahn replied. "Now, you mentioned the Communists. I'm very familiar with Marxist terrorism. As you've probably noticed from my accent, I'm a German national. In my country we've had considerable trouble from such groups as the Baader-Meinhoff Gang, the Second June Movement and the German Red Army faction. However, there have also been terrorist acts committed by the right-wing Turkish Gray Wolves and other small but nasty neofacist groups. What's interesting is, in most cases, the Soviet KGB was influencing or manipulating the terrorists. *Both* left-wing and right-wing groups."

"That doesn't seem very logical," Captain Whitney said, frowning.

"Terrorists are fanatics," the German continued. "They're crazy little groups, consisting of small numbers of extremists. These groups could never literally overthrow the government of a large, powerful country. The Soviets know this and they don't expect the terrorists to accomplish such tasks. All they expect terrorists to do is cause some destruction, create fear, unrest and eventually dissatisfaction with the government in power at the time."

"True," Katz agreed. "And it doesn't make any difference if the terrorists involved are left-wing or right-wing. Either way, they're cannon fodder and pawns, used to set the stage for revolution in the future."

"I'm sorry," van Schooer said with a sigh. "I don't see how that applies in this case or how this links the kidnappings with the murders."

"The same principles may be involved here," Hahn explained. "Lincoln and Finley are kidnapped, attracting more unfavorable attention to South Africa. Influences and pressures from the U.N. increase. Then some murders occur. Terrorist-style murders of police officers and a Brazilian-death-squad-style killing of a member of an antiapartheid group... or so they thought."

"Divide and conquer," McCarter added. "Get both sides to fight with each other. Meantime, none of South Africa's allies will be willing to speak on her behalf because of the stink about Finley and Lincoln. An ideal situation for a revolution. The Soviets put their chums in power and Moscow claims the crown jewel of Africa. The whole continent would be in their control then.''

"There's only one thing that bothers me about this notion," Katz remarked, blowing a circle of smoke toward the ceiling. "Everything is happening too fast for this to be a typical KGB operation. The Soviets are usually very careful, and they tend to take some time with covert operations to avoid reckless mistakes."

"Could be some eager beaver hot for a promotion," James suggested. "Wouldn't be the first time a Russian commander jumped the gun and ordered his men to act too soon."

"Perhaps the Soviets aren't involved at all," Katz mused. "It's a bit too early to say for certain. However, our opponents seem to be displaying a pattern. If we can anticipate what they'll do next, we might be able to turn the tables on the bastards."

"That sounds very encouraging, Mr. Wallburg," Sergeant Major Oktoba remarked. "But the pattern doesn't seem very clear to me. How can we second-guess these bandits without having a better idea of what they're up to?"

"And don't forget Finley and Lincoln," Captain Whitney added. "The longer we waste time here debating this situation, the less likely we'll ever find those two alive."

"We're eager to go into action, mate," David McCarter assured the captain. "But before we kick arse, we have to make sure we aim our boots at the right backsides."

"Well," Katz said, "it's getting late and we could all use some sleep. Let's get some rest and tackle this problem in the morning. Perhaps inspiration will come to us in our dreams."

"Hoping for occult assistance, Mr. Wallburg?" Oktoba inquired with a grin.

"Right now," the Phoenix Force commander replied, "I would welcome any kind of assistance from any source."

10

The morning did not bring new inspiration, but it did present an unexpected and disturbing revelation. Pieter van Schooer returned to the safe house and awakened the men of Phoenix Force. The five commandos climbed from their cots, bleary-eyed with less than four hours' sleep. Yet they had obviously gotten more rest than the weary van Schooer.

"Sorry to wake you," the Afrikaner stated. "But this is too important to wait."

"I've got something to do that can't wait, either," David McCarter growled as he headed for the bathroom. "Just don't run off to war while I'm in the loo."

"When you gotta go," Calvin James commented, "you gotta go."

"I think the rest of us can hold our kidneys long enough to hear what you've got to tell us," Yakov Katzenelenbogen told van Schooer as he sat on the edge of his cot. The Israeli wore an undershirt that revealed the naked stump of his right arm. The abbreviated limb simply ended at the elbow.

"A cassette tape was sent to the headquarters of Internal Security," van Schooer explained, trying not to stare at Katz's stump. "The tape contains a statement by Senator Finley."

"Then he's still alive," James mused.

"At least he was when the tape was made," Gary Manning corrected.

Time Bomb

"If the tape is genuine," Karl Hahn commented. Part espionage agent and part scientist, suspicion was deeply woven into Hahn's personality. "Do you have samples of Finley's voiceprint so the tape can be checked to be certain it is not a forgery?"

"That's already been done," van Schooer said with a nod. "The tape is genuine. Would you gentlemen like to hear it?"

"Naturally," Katz replied as he gathered up his prosthesis. The mechanical arm reminded van Schooer of a limb for a department store dummy. Yet the device had seemed quite lifelike when Katz wore the prosthesis and covered the metal arm with a sleeve.

The Afrikaner inserted a cassette tape into a Sony recorder. He glanced up from the machine to watch Katz fit the prosthesis to the stump. The Phoenix Force commander strapped the device firmly to the stubby limb, using his single hand and teeth. None of the other members of Phoenix Force offered assistance. Katz did not need any help. The prosthesis was attached within seconds. The steel hooks opened and closed as the Israeli tested the equipment to make certain it was operating correctly.

An unsteady voice with a New England accent spoke from the tape machine. The voice quivered with fear and occasionally stammered.

"This is Senator Thomas Finley," the voice announced. "The Reverend Robert Lincoln and I are being held by the People's Arm of Justice. We shall be kept here, prisoners of the war for equality, hostages for the cause of racial freedom, until the dictators of South Africa abolish the policy of apartheid and relinquish control of the government to appointed leaders from the United Democratic Front and the Free All South Africans organization. Only then will the republic have a just majority rule."

The men of Phoenix Force listened carefully, trying to detect any background sounds that might betray the location of the kidnappers. There were none.

"The following demands must be met," Finley's voice continued. "All whites must resign from office. A committee of officials from the UDF and FASA will later select white individuals to represent the interests of the white minorities of South Africa. All white landowners must surrender their property to the state. The land will be operated by the government and used for the benefit of all South Africans. The large corporations, also run by rich Afrikaners, must be dissolved. These businesses will also be turned over to the state and operated for the good of all. This community ownership and equal distribution of goods and services will create the needed social reforms within the republic. The wealth of the white oppressors will be confiscated and redistributed equally to the people."

"The Communist version of utopia," Karl Hahn commented.

"Yeah," Gary Manning added. "Sounds great in theory, but it's just another form of tyranny in practice."

"Finally," Finley's voice continued, "the Republic of South Africa will officially change its name to Hurumoyo. If these demands are not accepted within one week after receiving this message, Reverend Lincoln and I will be executed."

"That's it," van Schooer announced. "The rest of the tape is blank. No background noises. No voices. Nothing."

"Perhaps if the tape is amplified," Hahn suggested, "there may be sounds that cannot be detected with the human ear."

"Our lab personnel are working on that," the Afrikaner replied as he switched off the Sony. "However, we don't have much hope there. The kidnappers aren't making many mistakes. For example, there were no fingerprints on the original cassette—this is a copy, by the way. They're still working on the original, hoping to find some sort of clue."

"Heard the tail end of that tape," David McCarter commented as he fired up a Player's cigarette. "Anything at the beginning besides a buildup to a lot of damn fool demands?''

"Outrageous demands," van Schooer growled. "Those bastards can't honestly believe we'll agree to that nonsense."

"Of course they realize the government won't agree to their demands," Katz stated. "That means the kidnappers plan one of two strategies. First, they've made the most excessive demands possible and plan to negotiate terms with the government. Typical horse-trading. Haggle over the terms until both sides come to an agreement."

"Negotiate with kidnappers and blackmailers?" Van Schooer shook his head. "My government will never agree to that."

"Maybe not," Manning commented. "But governments make deals all the time with kidnappers, blackmailers, terrorists and mass murderers. Of course, those guys are usually in politics so they're referred to as statesmen, instead."

"The kidnappers might be trying to blackmail you into terms," Katz said. "But that's still better than the other possibility."

"Which is?" van Schooer inquired.

"They intend to kill Finley and Lincoln," the Phoenix Force commander replied. "In fact, they may have already done so. You see, the demands are so extreme they know your government won't agree to them. However, the terrorists have now given you an option that could, in theory, save the lives of two Americans held hostage. When your government refuses to agree to these terms and the prisoners are executed, a great many people will feel that the fault lies with your government for being inflexible instead of with the kidnappers who are fighting for their 'noble cause.' ''

"That's absurd," the Afrikaner declared. "Do you think we should agree to this extortion? Surrender our country to those damn Communists?"

"No," Katz assured him. "But the rest of the world tends to look at South Africa and see nothing but apartheid. Just as most people looked at Rhodesia and saw only racial discrimination and segregation. Those same people don't bother to look at what's happened since Rhodesia became Zimbabwe, and they don't criticize the government in power there. They figure the white minority is out of power and the black majority is in. That satisfies their sense of justice. Very few will look at the results in Zimbabwe."

"It was that way after the British left Uganda," McCarter added. "People figured the country was free and had self-government. It wasn't until Idi Amin launched attacks on other countries and kidnapped a planeload of Israelis at Entebbe that anyone cared what sort of dictatorship that bastard was running."

"Yeah," James said, sighing. "Black dictators can be just as bad as white dictators."

"But they usually don't get as much criticism," Hahn remarked. "Especially from the United Nations. Three-fourths of the countries represented at the U.N. are Communist regimes or Third World nations, often with Marxist overtones. The United Nations will be very critical of South Africa if Finley and Lincoln are killed."

"The U.S. won't be very understanding, either," Katz added. "South Africa will be subjected to considerable pressure from all directions, and you won't have too many allies. If the Communists and SWAPO decide to launch a full-scale invasion, you won't be able to count on anyone to help you. Even Israel might back off from such a volatile situation."

"Then we have no choice." The Afrikaner sighed. "We'll have to launch raids on the headquarters of the United Democratic Front and the Free All South Africans organization. Members will be interrogated and their buildings and homes searched for evidence."

"Jesus Christ." James rolled his eyes toward the ceiling. "Don't you know what sort of turmoil that could cause?

Man, that would cause riots and bloodshed worse that anything this country has ever seen.''

"I appreciate the risks involved,'' van Schooer assured
him. "But what other choice do we have? Surrender to the
demands of these thugs? I'm certain you don't approve of
apartheid, Mr. Walker, but I had hoped you would not approve of abolishing it through blackmail.''

"I've already told you what I think,'' James snapped.
"Of course I think apartheid is wrong, and regardless of
what you say, I think more can be done to do away with it.
But I don't want to see your country turned into another
Zimbabwe or Angola. I don't want to see black and white
South Africans killing each other because your govern-
ment can't find some goddamn kidnappers.''

"I agree with Walker,'' Katz stated. "Besides, raiding the
antiapartheid centers and harassing their supporters might
be playing right into the hands of the enemy.''

"That's right,'' Hahn agreed. "They might be trying to
stir up a hornets' nest between the antiapartheid people and
your government. We really don't know who is behind this
People's Arm of Justice.''

"They want the present government dissolved and replaced with persons from the two major antiapartheid
groups,'' the Afrikaner declared. "That makes the guilty
party rather obvious.''

"Not necessarily,'' McCarter commented. "The kidnappers are asking for a lot more than simply abolishing
apartheid. And isn't it a bit odd that the tape didn't include
Lincoln's voice as well as Finley's?''

"Finley is obviously reading his message,'' Katz said.
"The kidnappers prepared it for him. Lincoln may have
been killed already or otherwise unable to speak.''

"But if the proapartheid forces are really responsible,''
the Briton mused, "would they be more apt to kill a black
American than a white one?''

"Maybe Lincoln caused more of a fuss," James said with a shrug. "Mr. van Schooer, is Swahili widely spoken in South Africa?"

"Not really," the Afrikaner answered. "The two official languages of the republic are Afrikaans and English. However, numerous black African languages are spoken here, mostly Zulu and Xsopha. Of course, people have migrated to our country from virtually every other African country, so we've got a lot of Swahili-speaking people as well."

"Well," James began, "I don't claim to understand Swahili fluently, but *hurumoyo* means 'free heart' unless I'm getting my words confused. Why would the anti-apartheid people want to give South Africa a new name in a language that isn't spoken by the majority of people who live here?"

"Don't forget," Manning warned, "one of those guys we met at the FASA headquarters spoke Swahili."

"I didn't forget," James assured him. "That's why I think we'd better go back there and have a talk with Cromo and his friends. Let them know what's going on and get their side of this business."

"Do you think they'd tell you the truth if they were involved in the kidnapping?" van Schooer asked dryly.

"Probably not," James admitted. "But we're sitting on a political time bomb. If it explodes a lot of people, black and white, will be hurt. The final result of that explosion will either be a violent takeover of South Africa, probably controlled by the Reds, or the present government will become more repressive and less trusting of blacks. I don't want either to happen to your country."

"I appreciate that," the Afrikaner said with a nod. "But going to the FASA center is dangerous. Remember what happened yesterday?"

"My memory isn't that short I'd forget," the black man assured him. "Risk is part of the job, and I'm willing to take it."

"But this time you're getting some backup," Katz declared.

"If we show up with half a dozen guys packing heavy artillery, that could trigger trouble from the start," James complained.

"Backup, Mr. Walker," the Israeli repeated. "That means two or three of us go in and the others stay in the background, ready to come to our aid if necessary."

"*Our* aid?" James raised his eyebrows. "You planning to go in with me?"

"Yes," Katz confirmed. He turned to Manning. "You're our best rifle marksman, you're the logical choice for a long-range backup in an emergency."

"Kruger and I aren't going to be left out of this party, are we?" McCarter asked. The British war machine was obviously eager to go into battle.

"You won't be left out," Katz assured him. "But don't forget, this isn't an assault on an enemy camp. For all we know, Cromo and the FASA might be perfectly innocent."

"Have I ever shot anyone when it wasn't necessary?" McCarter replied.

"Not that we know of," Manning muttered. "But there's always a first time."

"You're the one who likes to go up to Canada and shoot defenseless moose," the Briton told him. "They can't shoot back."

"Moose have antlers," Manning said with a shrug.

PHOENIX FORCE ARRIVED at the Johannesburg headquarters of Free All South Africans. Sergeant Major Oktoba drove a VW Golf with Calvin James and Yakov Katzenelenbogen in the back seat. As they approached the FASA building, a long blue vehicle appeared in the rearview mirror. James was startled by the bulging headlights and canvas roof above a rectangular windshield. He turned in his seat to get a better look at the ancient 1925 Austin.

"Man," James remarked. "Would you look at that old car? Like something out of a gangster movie on the late show, huh?"

"Yes," Katz said dryly. "That's what cars used to look like when I was a boy."

"You'll see quite a few old cars on the roads in South Africa, my friends," Oktoba announced. Unlike the late Sergeant Muspula, Oktoba always seemed cheerful and eager to chitchat. "There are even some Studebakers and Model T Fords puttering about. I even saw a De Dietrich once. That car must be close to eighty years old."

"Oh-oh," James rasped when he noticed two young black men standing in front of the FASA building. Both held double-barreled shotguns. "Those dudes don't look too friendly today."

"If they raise those guns it'll be the last mistake they'll ever make," Katz commented, glancing down at the walkie-talkie on the lid of his briefcase beside him.

The Israeli gathered up the transceiver and pressed the transmit button. "Eagle One to Eagle Two," he spoke into the mouthpiece. "Do you read me? Over."

"Read you, Eagle One," Gary Manning's voice replied from the radio. "The reception committee is packing iron today. Over."

"We noticed, Eagle Two," Katz assured him. "Pass the word to Eagle Three. I'm going to switch off my radio. These people are already jumpy. I don't want them to see me talking on this thing and start worrying what we might be up to. Over."

"Affirmative, Eagle One," the Canadian told him. "By the way, I spotted at least two figures with weapons at windows so far. Watch yourselves. Over."

"Thanks," Katz replied. "Over and out."

He laid down the radio. The Phoenix Force commander patted the lid to his attaché case. The luggage contained an Uzi submachine gun with a folding stock and two M-26 fragmentation grenades. Katz also carried his SIG-Sauer pistol in shoulder leather and a .380 Beretta in a holster at the small of his back. James was carrying his Colt Commander in the Jackass Leather shoulder rig with the G-96 Jet Aer dagger under his right arm.

Oktoba steered the Volkswagen onto the driveway and parked the car a few yards from FASA headquarters. The sentries stiffened, but did not raise their scatterguns. James and Katz emerged from the Golf. The Israeli held the attaché case, the hooks of his prosthesis clamped around the handle.

"You plan to do some trapshooting today?" James remarked, gesturing at the guards' shotguns.

"I remember you," one of the sentries remarked. "You're the nigger from America, right? Where'd you find this old cripple?"

"Does FASA teach lessons in rudeness or did you learn vulgar remarks in your spare time?" Katz inquired.

"I think the kid's still recovering from a lobotomy," James said with a shrug. "Look, fella, I'm sure we could enjoy this sparkling conversation all day, but we need to talk to Phillip Cromo."

"You talked to him yesterday," the guard said with a snicker. "He doesn't want to talk to anyone today."

"He'd better change his mind," Katz warned. "A tape recording arrived at the Internal Security headquarters today...."

"*Arrived* there?" the sentry muttered through clenched teeth. "Don't you mean it was *sent* from there?"

"What are you talking about?" Katz asked.

"You know what I'm talking about," the sentry replied.

"If he knew he wouldn't ask, asshole," James snapped. "Now tell Cromo if he doesn't want a lot of innocent people to get killed, he'd better talk to us."

"You're full of shit," the sentry growled.

Suddenly, a military deuce-and-a-half truck roared up the driveway. The vehicle skidded to a halt as uniformed figures jumped from the back of the rig. The soldiers swung the muzzles of their submachine guns toward Katz and James.

11

The men of Phoenix Force were ultraprofessionals. Their reflexes had been honed by years of intensive training and experience. Calvin James and Yakov Katzenelenbogen dived to the ground before the gunmen opened fire. Four streams of full-auto projectiles sliced air above the prone bodies of the two supercommandos. The two FASA sentries were not as fortunate.

Bullets crashed into the bodies of the guards and they executed a grotesque spasmodic dance. One sentry raised his shotgun and triggered a burst of buckshot into the sky before both men fell back against the door, blood smearing the surface as their twitching forms slumped lifeless to the porch.

"Son of a bitch," Gary Manning rasped as he watched the carnage through the Bushnell scope mounted to the frame of his FN *Fusil Automatique Léger*—Light Automatic Rifle.

The Canadian Phoenix pro was stationed on the roof of the Fordsburg-Johannesburg Trust and Savings, four hundred yards from the FASA headquarters building. Manning had seen the truck approach the home base of the antiapartheid organization and immediately gathered up his FAL rifle in case something went sour. He had seen the four soldiers jump from the vehicle and start shooting. They would have cut down Katz and James if the Phoenix Force pair had failed to duck fast enough.

Manning was not certain if the uniformed killers were enemy agents in disguise or genuine troops. At the moment, he did not give a damn. Two of his teammates were in trouble. That made the gunmen the enemy, regardless of who they were. The cross hairs of the Bushnell scope found the back of a gunman's head and the Canadian squeezed the trigger.

A 3-round burst smashed into the killer's skull. The high-velocity 7.62 mm blasted the gunman's skull apart as if it were a melon struck by a sledgehammer. He collapsed to the ground, brains spilling from his shattered cranium.

Only one of the other gunmen noticed his comrade had been shot. The other two were concentrating on training their weapons on the prone figures of Calvin James and Yakov Katzenelenbogen. James, however, had already drawn his Colt Commander and held the pistol in a firm two-handed grip. The black warrior snap-aimed at the closest opponent and fired the big handgun.

The gunman cried out as a Silver-Tip hollowpoint slug punched into his solar plexus. The powerful 185-grain projectile snapped the xiphoid process, located at the posterior of the sternum, traveled upward and punctured a lung. James fired the Colt again and pumped a second .45-caliber round into the man's chest. The bullet smashed bone and tunneled into the killer's heart. The gunman's Beretta M-12S submachine gun tumbled from his hands as he fell to the ground and died.

Another uniformed assassin was about to blast James and Katz with a British-made Sterling subgun. He might have succeeded if Sergeant Major Oktoba had failed to fire his Sanna carbine quickly enough.

Oktoba squeezed off three Parabellum rounds as fast as he could work the trigger, and the sergeant major's bullets slammed into the gunman's back, all three drilling the bastard between the shoulder blades. The killer's spinal cord snapped like a frayed rope. The man half turned from the impact of the multiple 9 mm slugs and triggered his Sterling chattergun, firing a burst of harmless projectiles into the ground. Then he dropped in a quivering lump, his life seeping from his body faster than a politician can break his promises.

The fourth gunman had hesitated, uncertain if he should run for cover to flee from Manning's rifle or help his comrades fight James and Katz. Suddenly, he found himself alone. The other three triggermen were already dead. The nearest threat appeared to be Calvin James, who held a smoking pistol in his fists. The gunman turned his Beretta chopper toward the black commando.

Something struck the buttonman in the side of the head. The object was not large, but it hit hard and fast. So fast, it seemed to burn through his brain like a bolt of hot metal. This was his last sensation before he died. The man never heard the report of Manning's rifle.

Two more subgun-packing killers jumped from the back of the truck as the driver stomped on the gas pedal to hastily retreat from the scene. Four more men were in the back of the deuce-and-a-half, but they elected to remain inside the rig. If their gung-ho buddies wanted to get killed trying to avenge the deaths of the first hit team, that was their problem. The men inside the truck were veteran survivors, who did not believe in sticking their necks out without a good reason.

However, the two eager-beaver buttonmen did not have to face Phoenix Force alone. Five more gunmen, dressed in civilian clothing and carrying either submachine guns or handguns, rushed from the ancient Austin automobile to assist their comrades. Not surprisingly, they were upset when the truck started to speed away from the battlefield.

"You bastards!" a gunman shouted as he fired his Beretta M-12 at the retreating vehicle.

Two attackers prepared to waste Katz and James with their subguns. However, Yakov had taken his Uzi from the briefcase and snapped the wire stock into position. He braced the compact submachine gun across his prosthesis and opened fire before the killers could use their weapons. The Israeli war-horse raked his opponents with a volley of 9 mm hell, expertly blasting the pair into oblivion. Their bullet-riddled bodies wilted to the ground.

The sharp *crack* of medium-caliber rifles snarled from the windows of the FASA building. An enemy gunman shrieked as a bullet from an antiapartheid rifleman plowed into his groin. The man tumbled to the ground, thrashing about in agony and clawing at what remained of his testicles. Another gunman cried out when a rifle slug smashed into his triceps and splintered bone. He fell to his knees, clutching his wounded arm.

An aggressor raised his Sterling blaster and sprayed the windows with 9 mm rounds. Glass shattered and wood chips burst from windowsills. A FASA defender clamped both hands to his bullet-crushed face. Blood seeped between his fingers as he slumped to the floor.

Calvin James aimed his Colt at the creep who was still hosing the building with Parabellum slugs. The Phoenix warrior aimed carefully and squeezed the trigger. A .45-caliber missile struck the gunman in the back of the knee, and the big hollowpoint projectile burst the joint apart. The hit man howled and fell on his back. James fired his Commander again. The second bullet crashed into the wounded gunsel's arm and shattered his elbow. The hapless goon screamed again and fainted.

Another gunman turned his attention and the aim of his Sterling toward Sergeant Major Oktoba at the VW Golf. The BSS agent raised his Sanna carbine, but he realized he was not quick enough. The best Oktoba could hope for was to take the bastard with him.

Suddenly, the gunman's face exploded as a 7.62 mm slug burst from the center of his forehead. The trigger man fell forward, the back of his skull split by a deep bullethole. Oktoba sighed with relief and glanced up at the Phoenix Force version of a guardian angel—Gary Manning with a sniper rifle.

The last aggressor had also noticed the Canadian, who now stood boldly on the roof of the Fordsburg-Johannesburg Trust and Savings. Manning lowered his FAL and stared down at the gunman. Snarling, the terrorist raised his Beretta M-12 and fired a burst of 9 mm hornets at the Phoenix Force marksman.

But the compact, short-barreled Beretta subgun was designed for close-quarters combat. Manning was out of range. The enemy Parabellum rounds whined sourly as the projectiles fell short of their target and ricocheted off the brick wall of the bank beneath Manning's feet. The Canadian calmly put the stock of his Belgian rifle to his shoulder and peered through the Bushnell scope. He squeezed the trigger and fired three 7.62 messengers into the center of the gunman's chest. The guy went down hard and never got up again.

THE ENEMY TRUCK did not get far. David McCarter and Karl Hahn confronted the fleeing vehicle before it could travel two blocks. Phoenix Force had anticipated possible trouble from the FASA, but they had not expected the more than two dozen mysterious and well-armed gunmen who attacked from a different direction.

McCarter and Hahn charged from their cover behind a small grocery market. The Briton's favorite combat piece hung from a shoulder strap by his right hip—an Ingram M-10 machine pistol, a compact boxlike killing machine capable of dealing out Parabellum death at 1000 rounds per minute. The M-10 is a short-range weapon, but McCarter did his best work at close quarters.

The Briton held an SAS "flash-bang" grenade in his right fist and prepared to pull the pin, while Karl Hahn aimed a Heckler & Koch MP-5 at the advancing truck. The driver of the vehicle stomped on the gas, hoping to run the pair over. His passenger drew a Browning automatic from shoulder leather and extended his arm out the window to fire at the two Phoenix Force crusaders.

Hahn triggered a long burst of 9 mm slugs, raking the windshield with high velocity missiles. Three or four Parabellums punched through the thick concave glass. Two bullets bored into the chest of the pistolman, chopping his heart to pulp. A third round smashed the driver's right shoulder joint. The man screamed and fell against the steering wheel and the truck swerved as McCarter hurled the grenade.

The British ace lobbed the miniblaster under the truck, and when the grenade exploded a fierce concussion blast lifted the vehicle and turned it over on its side. The truck crashed down on a concrete sidewalk and skidded into a lamppost. Terrorists poured out of the back of the deuce-and-a-half like angry wasps from a ruptured nest.

Before any of the gunmen could aim their weapons, McCarter opened fire with his M-10. The Briton expertly hosed the enemy troops, chopping 9 mm devastation into the upper torso of one gunsel and blasting apart the lower jawbone and teeth of another. With both lungs and heart crushed by 115-grain projectiles, the first man had no choice but to drop to the pavement and die. The second terrorist dropped his Sterling subgun and desperately groped at his lower face. His hands found nothing but ragged flesh, splintered bone and blood. Lots of blood. A bullet had severed his carotid artery. The horrified triggerman could not scream, so he simply passed out and fell to the sidewalk, his life spilling out in crimson spurts.

A third terrorist ducked around the side of the truck, seeking shelter from McCarter's Ingram. He scurried for shelter, working the bolt of his Beretta blaster as he ran. The gunman stopped abruptly when he found himself staring into the muzzle of Karl Hahn's H&K machine pistol.

The terrorist decided he had one chance to take out Hahn. He raised his arms slowly, holding the Beretta M-12 at shoulder level. Hoping to catch the German off guard, he suddenly threw himself to the sidewalk and tried to point his weapon at Hahn and open fire. Hahn's H&K snarled before the gunman hit the pavement, and three Parabellums sent the terrorist tumbling across the sidewalk. Three more punched into his rolling body, mangling vital organs into lifeless mush.

"Scheisserkopf," Hahn muttered with contempt.

The fourth and last gunman to emerge from the back of the truck raised his hands overhead in surrender. He addressed McCarter in a trembling combination of rapid French and broken English.

"Non shoot, *s'il vous plaît*!" the man pleaded. *"Non arme à feu.* Understand?"

"Oui," McCarter assured him. *"Ne bougez pas!"*

The French terrorist did not intend to move. He stood as still as a statue while McCarter carefully stepped closer to peer inside the rear of the truck to be certain no more opponents lurked there. The back of the rig was empty, but hinges creaked at the cab of the vehicle. Metal struck metal and a voice groaned loudly. McCarter stepped back to peer around the truck to see what caused the noise.

The Frenchman took advantage of the distraction and leaped forward, lashing a roundhouse kick to McCarter's Ingram. The terrorist's boot connected hard, striking the M-10 from the Briton's hands. The savate-trained hoodlum pivoted sharply and swung a high wheel kick, aiming the back of his left heel at McCarter's face.

The Briton slammed his right forearm into the back of his opponent's knee, and the attacker's leg buckled before he could complete the kick. McCarter's boot snapped a vicious kick between the man's splayed legs. The terrorist wheezed like a dying horse as the terrible pain exploded in his genitals and shot through his nervous system.

"Bleedin' arse hole," McCarter growled as he punched his opponent in the kidney.

The terrorist groaned. His head snapped back as his body convulsed with fresh agony. McCarter quickly clapped the open palms of both his hands against the sides of the Frenchman's skull. The thug's eardrums burst, and another wave of pain swept through him. The terrorist sighed, almost relieved to finally sink into unconsciousness.

"Are you all right?" Karl Hahn inquired as he marched a wounded enemy trooper from the front of the truck. The captive held his left hand on top of his head. His right arm dangled limply from a bullet-ravaged shoulder.

"Just had to teach a bloke some fine points about the manly art of dirty fighting," the Briton replied cheerfully. "I see you managed to take a prisoner."

"This is our 'hot-rodder,'" Hahn answered. "Is that expression still used in America?"

"How would I know?" McCarter said with a shrug.

"I am an American citizen," the terrorist announced, his Alabama accent distorted as he spoke through clenched teeth. "I wanna speak to the U.S. embassy...."

"Let me guess," Hahn said, "you're with the Peace Corps, right?"

"I ain't tellin' you fuckers nothin'," the captive muttered.

"You'll talk, mate," McCarter replied with a wolfish grin. "By the time we're finished with you, you're going to tell us things you didn't even realize you knew."

12

"Will someone please tell me what's going on?" Phillip Cromo asked as he limped from the Free All South Africans headquarters building.

"We're trying to put the pieces together, too," Yakov Katzenelenbogen confessed, still holding the Uzi subgun in his fist. "But I think we'll have this puzzle solved soon."

"Who are you?" Cromo demanded. "I met that black American yesterday. I thought he was probably CIA, working with the government to try to harass us into a false confession concerning the kidnapping of Finley and Lincoln. But I don't know what to think of you now."

"Who we are isn't important," Katz replied. "We're not your enemies, and we're not working for the South African government."

"Obviously," Cromo said. "You helped defend us from these army butchers. My God! What will we do now? They'll send a regiment of Hippos to wipe us out!"

"I don't think the army sent them," Katz told him. "If they did, there was one hell of a snafu between the BSS and the military."

"BSS?" Cromo frowned. "But you said you're not working with the government."

"Not working *for* the government," the Phoenix Force commander corrected. "We're working with the BSS, just as we'd like to work with you."

"I don't think I'm going to like what you have to say," the FASA leader replied, glaring at Katz with his single eye.

"I radioed home base," Sergeant Major Oktoba announced as he approached the pair. "The police have been contacted and told to keep out of our business. Competent people are coming to help us haul out the dead and wounded."

"You're BSS?" Cromo said, referring to the security service as one might a loathsome disease. "A black man helping the whites to oppress other blacks...."

"This isn't the time to debate politics," Katz declared. "Except the politics of survival. I'm not talking about the survival of your group or the government of South Africa, but the very survival of your country."

"Hope you told them to send medical supplies and somebody to help stitch the wounded back together," Calvin James told Oktoba. "I've just about used up my first-aid gear."

"Oh, they'll help you treat the wounded white men," Cromo said with a snort. "A couple of my people were injured, and I'm certain the government won't care if they bleed to death."

"I'll take a look at them," James said wearily. "Meantime, why don't you quit bitching at Sergeant Major Oktoba? He helped us fight these sons of bitches, in case you didn't notice."

"No need to defend me, Walker," Oktoba said with a grin. "Mr. Cromo is welcome to his opinion of me. You're an Xsopho, correct, Mr. Cromo?"

"That's right," Cromo admitted. "You look like a Zulu, Oktoba, but your name is Swahili. What are you, besides a bootlicker for the Afrikaners?"

"My father was a Bantu and my mother was Zulu," the sergeant major answered. "They were both killed by the Xsopho sixteen years ago. Shall we discuss reasons for bitterness sometime, Mr. Cromo?"

"Some *other* time," Katz insisted. "You mentioned a tape recording, Mr. Cromo. Please explain."

"You don't know?" Cromo raised the eyebrow above his single eye. "Both the United Democratic Front and the FASA received cassette tapes of a statement by Reverend Robert Lincoln. He stated that agents for the white government are holding him hostage. He warned us that if we didn't cease protests about apartheid and discrimination in South Africa, the government would 'execute him for conspiracy against the rightful rulers of the republic.' Lincoln also urged us to stop supporting disinvestment and to terminate all connections with the Angolans, SWAPO and the African Congress Organization."

"I can understand opposition to apartheid," Oktoba remarked. "But you really should sever relations with those damn terrorists, Cromo."

"Please, Sergeant Major," Katz said. "Let's not discuss that now. The important thing is you received a tape of Lincoln that connects the kidnapping of Lincoln and Finley with the government. Yet Internal Security received a tape of Finley that connects the abductors with the antiapartheid movement."

"The government must have forced Finley to make that tape," Cromo decided. "They'll probably present the tape to the world press to try to convince everyone the antiapartheid groups are responsible for the kidnapping. The Lincoln tape is supposed to blackmail us into ceasing our protests."

"Man, that's ridiculous," James muttered. "South Africa hasn't been getting much sympathy from the rest of the world. Maybe they don't deserve much and maybe they've been getting a little more crap than they deserve—although apartheid is just plain wrong. No two ways about that."

"There is when you consider the fact the Xsopho and the Zulu are traditional enemies," Oktoba stated. "So are the Bantu and virtually none of us get along with Bushmen. If apartheid ended tomorrow, blacks would be killing blacks all over the republic. If we want equality, we'd better start by proving we can live with each other peacefully."

"The point I'm trying to make is that the government of South Africa wouldn't be stupid enough to think they could get away with the scheme you're suggesting, Cromo," James said quickly before Cromo could reply to Oktoba's remark. "After all, you don't intend to just accept the Lincoln tape and stop protesting apartheid, do you?"

"Of course not," Cromo confirmed. "I plan to meet with leaders of the United Democratic Front and perhaps Bishop Tutu in order to discuss how best to present this evidence to the world press."

"Naturally," Katz said. "And whoever sent you the tape must have predicted that would be your reaction."

"You don't expect us to just sit on this information, do you?" Cromo demanded.

"Until we can learn more about the kidnappers," the Phoenix Force leader urged. "It may not be too late to rescue Lincoln and Finley."

"The government has probably killed them by now," the FASA boss said with a shrug. "Besides, silence won't protect them from execution."

"Maybe not," David McCarter declared as he and Karl Hahn shoved two dazed captives toward the FASA building. "But it sure won't improve their chances for survival."

"Did you two discover something of interest?" Katz inquired.

"One of these blokes is an American and the other is French," McCarter answered. "Unless I'm guessing up the wrong occupation, I figure they're mercenaries."

"Mercenaries hired by the government to throw off suspicion," Cromo said, but he realized this statement made little sense even as he spoke.

"If these were black African mercenaries dressed as civilians, you might have a valid argument," Karl Hahn began. "But why would the government hire white mercenaries disguised as South African soldiers if they wanted to avoid suspicion?"

"But I can assure you neither the FASA or the United Democratic Front hired any mercenaries or kidnapped Senator Finley and Reverend Lincoln," Cromo insisted. "We were under attack, damn it!"

"This time," James replied. "But two police officers were killed yesterday, as well as Sergeant Muspula."

"What are you suggesting?" Cromo asked, totally confused.

"We believe someone is trying to manipulate your group and the United Democratic Front into more radical action against the government of South Africa," Katz explained.

"And vice versa," Karl Hahn added. "Our shadowy opponents are pitting you against each other, Mr. Cromo."

"I believe they speak the truth," Oktoba remarked to Cromo. "Although I doubted this theory until now, the attack on your headquarters is pretty convincing evidence. Unless, of course, some of your own people think you'd serve the cause better as dead martyrs than live protesters."

"That claim is too absurd to even consider," Cromo replied stiffly. "And I'll need more proof before I believe this 'sinister conspiracy' you speak of."

"Give us four hours," Katz urged. "Within that length of time, I promise you we will have proof of the manipulation by this mysterious group. The same group that has kidnapped Finley and Lincoln."

"What kind of proof?" the FASA leader asked, frowning.

"Why don't you join us and find out for yourself?" Calvin James invited. "Or send somebody you trust to report, if you're afraid we might be luring you into a trap."

"Perhaps I'll do that," Cromo replied.

"That's fine with us," Katz assured him. "But something else *must* be done immediately. You have to contact the United Democratic Front and explain what happened here. Convince them not to turn over the information from the Lincoln tape to the press until we've had enough time to get the information we need."

"Hey," the American terrorist spoke up in a trembling voice. "Just what the hell are you plannin' to do to get this information you're talkin' about?"

"Oh, you'll find out," McCarter said with a sinister chuckle. He swatted the back of a hand across the hoodlum's right biceps. "How's the shoulder, mate?"

The terrorist groaned and reached for his bloodied, bullet-smashed shoulder. Karl Hahn roughly shoved the barrel of his MP-5 under the man's left elbow to push the arm overhead.

"Nobody told you to lower your hand," the German said harshly.

"Don't get nasty with our captives," Katz told his men. "Not yet anyway."

"Four hours, Cromo," James began. "How about it?"

"Very well," the FASA leader agreed. "We'll give you four hours to come up with something. When that time is up, we'll contact the press."

"Agreed," Katz said with a nod.

PHILLIP CROMO DID NOT ACCOMPANY Phoenix Force to the safe house, but he sent a representative he was certain he could trust. Angela Cromo, the FASA leader's daughter, was an attractive young woman. Her skin was the color of milk chocolate, her body tall and slender with full, rounded breasts and long legs. Her cheekbones were high and her mouth wide, with full lips and white even teeth.

Yet her appearance contained a fierceness that one would not usually associate with a woman who possessed the face and figure of a professional model. Her hair was clipped short and teased until it jutted from her skull in a forest of spikes. Her eyes were pale brown with flecks of green in the pupils, revealing distrust and anger rather than warmth. She barely spoke as she sat beside Calvin James in the back of a Hippo van.

"What's your sign?" James inquired.

''What's that supposed to mean?'' she demanded, glaring at the American.

''It's a joke,'' he replied. ''Forget it.''

''I'm not here to be entertained, Walker,'' Angela told him. ''I am here because I have a duty to perform for my father and for the liberation of my people.''

''I've got a job to do, too,'' James said with a shrug. ''That doesn't mean we have to be unpleasant about working together.''

''You're working with the government,'' Angela snapped. Her gaze turned toward Sergeant Major Oktoba. ''Just like this traitor to his own race.''

''If you don't like South Africa,'' Oktoba said with a smile, ''why don't you and your father and all the rest of you simply leave the country? Go live in Zimbabwe or Angola or any other country in Africa and see if conditions are better for black people.''

''This is our country, too,'' Angela insisted. ''We have a right to demand equality. South Africa boasts that its cities and technology are comparable to those of Europe and the United States. The republic wants to be accepted as part of the Western world, so it is fair to judge its racial policies by those standards.''

''Lady,'' James began, ''you didn't come along to be entertained and we didn't bring you to hear a debate about politics. Let's just relax until we get to our base and start questioning our captives. Okay?''

''No,'' she told him. ''It is not okay. You're an American. What do you know about South Africa? Are you aware that blacks and coloreds who work on farmland owned by whites are paid part of the wages in the form of cheap wine? Trucks haul huge tanks of this terrible wine to the plantations and cattle ranches. The workers become steadily more dependent on their masters as their alcoholism increases. What better way to kill the desire of laborers to better themselves than to turn them into drunkards. What do you call them in your country, winos?''

"That's what they're called," James replied evenly.

"Don't you understand that we have to make the world understand our plight?" Angela asked, staring into the Phoenix warrior's eyes. "That's why Bishop Tutu has traveled to your country urging disinvestment. If the South African government can't export gold and diamonds to your country, the economic effect on the republic will force the government to make social changes."

"Chief Minister Gatsha Buthelezi has also visited America," Sergeant Major Oktoba remarked. "He's the chief of the Zulu nation, Kwazulu. Buthelezi has tried to urge Americans not to participate in disinvestment because to do so is only going to hurt all South Africans—white and black alike. And when everyone has to suffer in South Africa, you can bet the black South Africans will suffer the most."

"But the only way..." Angela began.

"Thank God," James remarked when he gazed through a gunport and recognized the safe house. "We've arrived."

Phoenix Force climbed out of the various military vehicles that had helped transport the four terrorists who had survived the gun battle at the FASA headquarters. The power of the South African military and the influence of the Internal Security department had proved quite valuable to the commandos. These connections had enabled them to keep the police out of the area and block off the news reporters who had swiftly descended upon the scene.

However, critics of South Africa often exaggerate the power of the government to "restrict freedom of speech." The national and international press would certainly report the military involvement and probably start accusing the government of genocide before they had a chance to get any facts about the incident. Trying to convince the press to suppress a story for the sake of national security is usually a waste of time. Phoenix Force hoped they would be able to enlist the assistance of Cromo's group in time to formulate a version of the gun battle that would maintain security and also defuse rumors that could lead to violence by hot-headed individuals among either the antiapartheid camps or the proapartheid supporters.

Unfortunately, they had been forced to sacrifice the security of the safe house in the process. There was little time to waste, and taking the prisoners to a conventional military or government-operated prison for questioning was vetoed because the press would be waiting for them with TV cameras and long-range microphones. If the enemy learned a number of their hired guns had been brought in for interrogation, the lives of Senator Finley and Reverend Lincoln would be in even greater jeopardy.

"My God!" Pieter van Schooer exclaimed when Phoenix Force arrived with their captives. "Why did you bring these people here?"

"We couldn't find the YMCA on the street map," Gary Manning replied dryly as he dragged a stretcher carrying a wounded terrorist across the threshold of the TV repair shop.

"I'm gonna need some more morphine," James announced, hurrying to his medical supplies. "And get somebody in here who can help me with blood types, transfusions and treating these dudes for shock. The guy who caught a bullet in the gonads needs to go to a hospital pronto. If I inject any scopolamine in his veins, it'd kill him for sure."

"Scopolamine?" Van Schooer stared at James.

"It's a truth serum," the black commando said as he inserted the needle of a hypodermic syringe into a small vial of liquid. "The most potent drug of its kind."

"I know what it is," the Afrikaner assured him. "I also know it's considered to be very dangerous."

"So are terrorists," Katzenelenbogen remarked.

"Didn't the Geneva Convention ban the use of scopolamine?" Captain Whitney inquired. "Something about causing heart attacks, I believe."

"The Geneva Convention never got into truth serums," Karl Hahn replied. "Besides, we've only got four hours to get information out of these characters. That means there isn't time to question and cross-examine the prisoners, looking for body language to betray lies and such. There isn't time to deprive them of sleep to break them down, either.''

"There are only two ways to get information in a hurry,'' Katz added. "Drugs or torture. The former might be questionable morally, but the latter is certainly worse. Torture is against our principles. That's a point I want all your men to understand, too. If any of them tortures one of our prisoners, I will personally shoot the sadist between the eyes.''

"Only if you beat me to it,'' McCarter added. "Another problem with torture is a bloke will say anything to try to stop the pain. If he doesn't know something, he'll lie because he thinks it's what the torturers want to hear. Besides being immoral and brutal, torture is bloody unreliable.''

"I'll need to hook the subjects to a polygraph,'' James declared. "A lie detector registers blood pressure, heartbeat and all that shit. I want to be able to keep track of how the scopolamine affects each person. Too strong a dose could be fatal and too small a dose could be ineffective. The polygraph will also help us determine if someone is resisting the drug or lying under the influence.''

"Are you sure this will work?'' Captain Whitney asked.

"We've used scopolamine on captives before,'' Katz assured him. "Walker knows what he's doing. Whatever secrets our 'guests' are keeping from us won't remain secret very long.''

13

Tai Skrubu put the hand-rolled cigar to his lips. His personal manservant and bodyguard, Nyundo, struck a match and held the flame to his master's cigar. Skrubu puffed on the cigar and nodded his thanks to his chief enforcer.

"Asante, Nyundo," Skrubu said softly, drawing smoke deep into his lungs.

Nyundo bowed in reply. Lieutenant Colonel Juan Raul Marzo glanced up at the big muscle-bound servant. Nyundo's wide ebony face was lined with a network of small round scars. The scars formed two upside-down V marks on each cheek with a similar emblem tattooed on his forehead. Colonel Marzo had seen such self-inflicted scars before. They were the trademark of an obscure Bantu warrior sect known as the Brothers of the Lion.

Marzo noticed Nyundo had an Russian-made Stechkin machine pistol in a holster on his belt, yet still carried a long fighting lance with a heavy metal blade. The war lance was as much a symbol of the *Simba Elfu Ndugu* as the strange facial tattoos. Marzo wondered how Skrubu had managed to employ one of these rare, extremely fierce Bantu warriors. The sect was almost extinct. Generally found in the Congo region, the Brothers of the Lion had joined with other rebel forces, ironically known as *Simbas*, to battle the white Europeans in the early sixties. Later the sect turned against the Communist influence in the Congo.

Colonel Marzo was uncomfortable in the presence of Nyundo. Ten years ago, the big Bantu would probably have killed any Cuban who dared step within range of his deadly spear. But times change and so do governments, enemies and allies. Last year, Tai Skrubu was the president of the tiny nation of Mardaraja. Now he was a fugitive from the country he had once ruled. Always the opportunist, he had conceived a plan of action for South Africa that appealed to the Soviets, who lusted for control of the wealthiest and most technically advanced nation on the Dark Continent.

Unfortunately for Colonel Marzo, the Soviets' policy in Africa has always been "tell Castro to send some more Cubans to do the dirty work."

Thousands of Cuban troops have been sent to Africa over the past twenty years, and under the command of "Russian advisors," the Cubans helped train disgruntled black Africans in the philosophy and ideology of Marxism. This included crash courses in terrorism. The realities of communism were not part of the education. The Africans were taught that the Soviets had come to liberate Africa from white imperialistic oppressors simply because they were generous lovers of freedom. They were willing to arm the "people's revolution" with no strings attached.

Marzo was thirty-eight years old. He had spent most of the past eighteen years in Africa, usually stationed in Angola. In fact, Marzo was one of several thousand Cubans who had been ordered to apply for naturalized citizenship in Angola in the late spring of 1985. If the Soviets ever decided to pull out of Africa, probably to show the world they were not really interested in owning the continent, they would still have some Angolan-Cuban agents left in Africa. As legal citizens of Angola, the Cubans could serve the interests of Havana—and thus the interests of Moscow—without being accused of "occupying" the country.

Lieutenant Colonel Marzo had been a Communist since he was a teenager. Too long to consider himself as anything else, although he no longer had the fiery idealism of youth. He prided himself on being a professional soldier who followed orders and carried out every mission with absolute determination. He had decided that dedication was a virtue unto itself.

"Your Havana cigars are very good, Colonel," Skrubu declared. "I might smoke them as a regular habit when I become rich."

"We still have to determine how this plan of yours is going to work, Mr. Skrubu," Marzo replied. The Cuban spoke fluent Swahili and smatterings of several other African languages. He had done a lot of bargaining with wild-eyed revolutionaries and greedy would-be despots, but Tai Skrubu was different. The former president of Mardaraja was a cold-blooded businessman who would have willingly sold his wife, daughters and mother into slavery for thirty pieces of silver.

"My plan has worked well so far," Skrubu said simply. "I told you I could successfully kidnap Senator Finley and Reverend Lincoln. I also promised that I'd have the government of South Africa and the antiapartheid forces accusing each other of the crime. I have already completed phase two and phase three of my plan."

"Phase two?" Marzo raised his thick black eyebrows.

"Tape recordings of statements by Finley and Lincoln," Skrubu explained. "That was the easy part. Breaking their spirits was child's play. As I'm sure you know, Americans are soft and cowardly. We treated them like animals in a cage and deprived them of sleep for a mere forty-eight hours. They didn't even try to resist after that. Both of those capitalist weaklings read their statements into the tape recorder like good little boys reciting for a Sunday school play."

"I assume you sent the tape recordings to the South African government?" Colonel Marzo inquired.

"Only the Finley tape," Skrubu answered. "On it, he claims the antiapartheid forces are holding him hostage. The Lincoln tape was sent to FASA headquarters and an official of the United Democratic Front. Naturally, that tape blames the government for the kidnapping. You see, the

Afrikaners don't really give a damn about the life of a black man, and the antiapartheid groups aren't terribly concerned about the life of a white man. The choices were made based on which tape would get the best results from each group."

"I can see how this will increase unrest and confusion," Marzo said with a nod. "But it won't be enough to assure us of full-scale rebellion within South Africa."

"That brings us to phase three," the African declared. "This involves the assassinations of police and military among the whites and antiapartheid leaders among the blacks. This has already begun. Did you hear about the two police officers who were blown to pieces the other day? Keep listening to your radio, Comrade. You'll hear about an assault on the FASA headquarters by the white supremacist ruling class. Believe me, Colonel, the Republic of South Africa is ready to explode. When that happens, you and your comrades from Cuba and the Soviet Union will be able to march into the shambles and seize control with ease."

"I'm not convinced that you've done enough to assure us the government of South Africa will fall," the Cuban stated.

"Then we'll simply assassinate some more whites and blacks in the country," Skrubu replied with a shrug. "There will be bloody combat in the streets. If the whites win, they'll be too worn down to prevent a large invasion by you and your associates."

"What if the blacks win?" Marzo inquired.

"That would be a problem?" Skrubu laughed. "You've already got supporters among the outlawed Communist Party in South Africa, and many members of the antiapartheid movement are Marxists. The only real leadership can be removed. Some, like the Zulus, might side with the Afrikaners, and they'd be executed or exiled if the antiapartheid zealots win. However, the vast majority of blacks in South Africa, or anywhere else on the continent for that matter, lack the education and sophistication to actually manage a country."

"If you weren't black yourself," the Cuban remarked, "I might think you a racist, Mr. Skrubu."

"What's racist about admitting that African rulers keep their subjects ignorant and discourage their personal drive and development that could make leaders in the future?" Skrubu said with a shrug. "This is true about all African leaders, white or black. It is also true about you Communists and probably true of the leaders of all nations, to some degree. At any rate, this is an advantage to you and Mother Russia, Colonel. If the disgruntled black rebels overthrow the government, taking control of South Africa will be child's play."

"And this is what you're offering to sell us?" Marzo mused. "The foundations of a revolution."

"Don't tell me South Africa isn't a very attractive prize," Skrubu said, sighing and puffing on his cigar. "Don't tell me it isn't worth at least fifty million dollars to claim the wealthiest treasure in the entire continent and to terminate the only real opposition to communism within all of Africa."

"Your plan is very clever," Marzo remarked. "Yet very simple. Tell me, don't you think we could have managed something like this without your assistance?"

"Your Russian friends aren't terribly fond of risk," the African said. "They weren't willing to stick their necks out with a scheme as bold as mine."

"No offense," the Cuban began, "but boldness is often the path of the fool. Didn't it occur to you that rushing this revolution might be careless? A thousand things might go wrong with this plan."

"Nothing will go wrong," Skrubu assured him. "South Africa is going to fall. If you aren't interested in seizing control, someone else will do it."

"Of course." Marzo smiled. "You're talking about your little covert auction, correct?"

Skrubu gasped. Sucking cigar smoke into his throat, the African coughed. Colonel Marzo still smiled, pleased that he had caught the smug little bastard off guard.

"You didn't think we knew about that, Mr. Skrubu?" Marzo inquired. "I've been in military intelligence operations in Africa for almost two decades. Naturally, as a Cuban officer, I've been working with the Russian KGB. Between you and me, the Russians are pigs and I hate their guts. However, I must admit the Soviet spy network is very impressive. They've got agents and informers all over Africa. Trying to keep secrets from the KGB is like trying to keep secrets from God."

"I . . . I don't know what auction you're talking about, Colonel," Skrubu assured him.

"The auction to seize control of South Africa, of course," Marzo stated. "You covertly contacted the South-West Africa People's Organization and the government of Zimbabwe and invited them to participate in your little auction. Plan to sell the revolution to the highest bidder? I understand you even invited Colonel Khaddafi as a buyer."

"All right," Skrubu said, sighing. "I admit it. What's wrong with making as large a profit as possible, Colonel? I'm not some starry-eyed revolutionary or an idealistic moron who thinks international communism will one day become a utopian world of peace and equality. I'm interested in making money, Colonel. Now, is Moscow willing to pay or not?"

"Perhaps," the Cuban replied. "And perhaps not. After all, there's no reason for us to pay you. You're not in a position to carry out an invasion on your own. We can simply move in and take over after the South African government and social structure fall apart."

"What if SWAPO or Zimbabwe beat you to it?" Skrubu inquired. "Or Libya, for that matter."

"You really are amusing, Mr. Skrubu," Marzo said with a laugh. "SWAPO is controlled by my people. They can't take any ambitious action unless we approve it. Zimbabwe is too weak and too divided by civil strife to attempt a major military action. So you have only one customer, Skrubu. Namely, the Soviet-Cuban forces that I represent.''

"You forget about Libya,'' Skrubu said. "Colonel Khaddafi is certainly wealthy enough to pay me fifty million dollars, and he can supply enough manpower to invade the country after I've finished softening it up for him.''

"Do you think Khaddafi will dare to defy the Soviet Union if we tell him to mind his own business?'' Marzo asked. "He knows them well enough to respect their authority.''

"So you're holding all the cards?'' Skrubu said, leaning on the field desk. "Well, I assumed I'd be doing business with you people, anyway. The price is fifty million dollars. The money doesn't have to be in American currency, but I don't want Russian rubles or Cuban pesos. That would be a bit too obvious when I tried to spend it or exchange it. However, West German deutschmarks or Swiss francs are acceptable. I will also agree to partial payment in any combination of the three currencies and the rest paid in gold bullion or even gold bonds. The Soviets shouldn't have any trouble with that.''

"Fifty million dollars?'' Marzo shook his head. "What will you do if we refuse? Cancel the revolution? It's a bit late for that, isn't it?''

"Not at all.'' Skrubu smiled. "I've planned this operation for some time, Colonel. I've considered everything in advance. Including the treachery of Communist negotiations.''

The African rose from his chair and moved to the screen-covered entrance of his tent. Skrubu gestured at the walls of rock that surrounded the terrorist base. Several caves were located along the stone walls.

"Senator Finley and Reverend Lincoln are still held prisoner in one of those caves, Colonel,'' Skrubu announced. "If I released them and allowed the Americans to tell what really happened, the revolution would end before it could begin."

"You can't do that," Marzo said. "They've seen you, Skrubu. You even told them who you are. You'd be exposing yourself as a kidnapper to the world. You'll have to come up with a better bluff than that."

"I'm not bluffing," Skrubu assured him. "I'm already a fugitive, Colonel. There's a price on my head in Africa. I'm wanted for 'crimes against humanity' during my reign as president of Mardaraja. I've got nothing to lose by being accused of kidnapping."

"So the revolution might be canceled," Marzo said with a shrug. "The Soviets and my Cuban superiors weren't really delighted with your plan anyway, Mr. Skrubu. As I said before, you're rushing this business. Frankly, we'd just as soon wash our hands of the whole mess."

"Too late for that, Colonel." The African smiled. "You see, I've got a camera team stationed in one of those caves. They're equipped with long-range lenses that can photograph people from a quarter of a mile away. They also have a movie camera with a similar lens. In short, Colonel, there is now photographic proof that a Cuban intelligence officer has been conspiring with me. It's on film as well. Perhaps we'll have it put on videotape and offer 'The Cuban Connection' in VHS or Beta."

"Bastardo," Marzo muttered as he stood up. *"Qué la chigada!"*

Nyundo suddenly thrust his spear forward, aiming the blade at Marzo's chest. The Cuban raised his hands to assure the Bantu warrior that he did not intend to lose his temper. Skrubu laughed as he approached the desk.

"Technology is a wonderful thing, isn't it?" he remarked. "What's your decision, Colonel? Does Moscow want a scandal or do they want an opportunity to seize control of South Africa?"

"You really are a disgusting pig, Skrubu," Marzo said grimly. "And you have no idea of what you're getting into.

Trying to blackmail me is like inviting the KGB to hunt you down and kill you.''

"I'll worry about the Russians later," Skrubu replied. "Now, fifty million dollars or the whole world gets a very hot item about Communist conspiracies in Africa."

"Fifty million is too much," the Cuban stated. "I doubt if we'll be able to come up with more than ten million under the conditions you've set down."

"Thirty million," Skrubu insisted.

"Twenty," Marzo declared. "I'll try to convince the Soviets to agree to half of the payment in American, German, French or British currency."

"Not British," Skrubu corrected. "The pound isn't stable enough for my taste. Tell them to come up with at least five million in hard currency. No tricks. If I receive any counterfeit money, the deal is off."

"I'll do my best," Marzo agreed, "but I'll have to return to Angola and try to work out a deal with my superiors."

"I'll have you escorted to the border of Mozambique," Skrubu announced. "Of course, you'll have to be blindfolded, just as you were before being brought here. Security precaution. You understand, I hope?"

"Of course," Marzo muttered.

"Hopefully it won't take too long for you to fly to Angola and consult with your comrades," Skrubu declared. "I only intend to wait three days. Then I'll release Finley and Lincoln and deliver enough evidence to splash plenty of mud on the precious image of Cuba and the Russian Bear."

"I think we can come to an agreement in time," Marzo assured him. "Although you'll need more than photographs and film to condemn our actions in Africa."

"The photographs and film would probably be enough," Skrubu commented as he reached under the desk. "After all, you've been filmed with a known renegade and fugitive. However, I've got a extra bit of evidence."

The African pulled a small round metal object from the underside of the desk. He showed it to the Cuban colonel.

Marzo's face stiffened when he gazed down at the wireless microphone in Skrubu's hand.

"I'm certain you're familiar with devices such as this," Skrubu remarked. "The microphone transmits to a tape recorder located nearby. Naturally, we'll edit the tape a bit, copying only the statements that best incriminate you. Embarrassing remarks for your government and the Soviets in Africa. I'm afraid your superiors will probably treat you harshly if this material falls into the hands of the international media."

"Congratulations, Skrubu," Marzo said stiffly. "I really underestimated you."

"Just a bit of insurance," Skrubu assured him. "I thought it might encourage you to do your very best to convince the Communists to agree to my plan."

"I told you I'd do my best," Marzo stated. "And when this is over, I'll work just as hard to settle with you for this trick, Skrubu."

"I doubt that, Colonel," Skrubu said, smiling. "You're going to be too busy receiving medals and promotions after the People's Revolution claims South Africa as its newest victory."

"That remains to be seen, Skrubu," Colonel Marzo replied grimly.

14

"Gentlemen," Yakov Katzenelenbogen began. He turned to Angela Cromo and added, "And lady. It appears we've hit the jackpot."

"You learned where the enemy is holding Finley and Lincoln?" Pieter van Schooer asked eagerly.

The Afrikaner, Captain Whitney, Sergeant Major Oktoba and Angela Cromo had been waiting for more than three hours to hear the results of the interrogation of the captured terrorists. The men of Phoenix Force had insisted that they question the prisoners without anyone from either the South African government or the FASA being present. The commandos did not think any of their allies were involved with the terrorists, but they could not afford to take any risks.

Calvin James had administered scopolamine to two of the prisoners. The other captives were not physically fit to endure the powerful truth serum. Katz had helped James interrogate the pair. The process had taken some time to do correctly since they had to let the drug take effect, check the response of the person's body to scopolamine and ask questions slowly and precisely. Each subject had to be interrogated separately and cross-examined to make certain the answers remained consistent.

"We now have a general idea where the hostages are," Katz told the South Africans, taking a pack of Camel cigarettes from his shirt pocket. "Finley and Lincoln are being held in a remote valley, on the site of an abandoned mining project. They're still alive, or at least they were when Goodman last knew about them.''

"Goodman?'' Whitney inquired.

"One of the subjects we had a chat with,'' the Israeli explained, firing a cigarette with a battered Ronson lighter. "Arlon Goodman, a trigger-happy redneck from Alabama. He claims to be a sergeant in the private army of Major Kingston, a mercenary commander.''

"So my hunch was right,'' David McCarter commented. "These blokes are mercs. Didn't suspect they'd be Kingston's group, although I can't say I'm too surprised to hear it.''

"You're familiar with this Major Kingston?'' van Schooer inquired.

"I've never met the bastard,'' McCarter answered. "But I've heard of the son of a bitch. His real name is Jonathan Carlston, a former lieutenant in the Royal Marines. Sometime in the late sixties, Carlston became a mercenary. That doesn't bother me too much unless a chap doesn't give a damn about anything but money. Carlston has no principles, no morals and no sense of right or wrong. As long as he gets paid, he doesn't care who gets hurt during one of his missions. He's been involved in operations in Africa, the Middle East and probably South America.''

"How professional is he?'' Gary Manning inquired.

"From what I've heard, Carlston, or Kingston as he's calling himself now, is a better strategist than the average bandit leader,'' the Briton stated. "But I doubt that he's terribly clever. Kingston is bold and ambitious, and nobody can accuse him of being a coward. His greatest ability might be his knack for handling other unprincipled scum and getting them to follow orders.''

"Goodman certainly won't win any humanitarian awards either,'' Katz said. "He seemed to think humiliating Finley and Lincoln was a lot of fun. Goodman also claims to have personally participated in kidnapping the two Americans.''

"Who hired these mercenaries?" Whitney asked. "The Communists? A political extremist group?"

"That's the real surprise," Katz announced. "The mastermind behind the kidnapping and the recent terrorist activity is none other than Tai Skrubu, former president of Mardaraja."

"Well, I'll be damned." McCarter smiled. "Sort of ironic, isn't it?"

"How's that?" Angela asked.

"He means it's ironic we were thinking of just about every other possibility," Manning said quickly.

Karl Hahn smiled. He remembered the spectacular raid on the Mardarajan embassy in London. The German had thought at the time that the five mysterious invaders might have been Phoenix Force. Now he was sure of it.

"Where is this abandoned mine?" van Schooer began. "Let's get a strike force together and hit the sons of bitches."

"First we'll have to find out where the enemy stronghold is," Calvin James stated as he joined the others.

"But didn't this Goodman person tell you?" Angela asked, her ripe lower lip extended in a pout.

"He told us about the mine," James confirmed. "But neither Goodman or Hans Akerhole...or Akahome or whatever the name of the other is..."

"Akerhune," Katz supplied. "It's a Norwegian name. I only know about three or four hundred words in that language, and I'm glad he responded to French when we interrogated him."

"Yeah, the Asshole guy," James agreed. "Anyway, neither one of those dudes actually knows how to get to the place where Finley and Lincoln are held captive. They've both been there, but they can't tell us how to find it."

"What?" Van Schooer glared at James. "Are you sure that drug of yours worked on them?"

"They're telling the truth," Katz assured the Afrikaner. "It seems Skrubu is very security conscious. He doesn't trust the mercenaries in Kingston's command so he insists the mercs be blindfolded while traveling to and from the headquarters at the mine. Skrubu has a personal guard of black African Bantu troops and these fellas drive the mercs to and from Kingston's camp.''

"Kingston's camp?'' Captain Whitney raised his eyebrows. "So the mercenaries have a separate base of operations?''

"That's what Goodman and Akerhune told us,'' Katz confirmed. "We've got a good description of the merc camp and how to get there.''

"Good,'' Oktoba declared. "So we've got a target at last.''

"Let's not charge in like a bull in a china shop,'' Gary Manning urged. "Bear in mind, the mercenaries are working for Skrubu. That means they've got communications with their boss. If we raid the merc camp and give them an opportunity to contact Skrubu, he'll kill Lincoln and Finley.''

"What the hell is Skrubu trying to prove?'' McCarter wondered aloud. "Unless he's part of something a lot bigger than anything our prisoners know about.''

"We can put the pieces together later and try to figure out what this mess has all been about,'' Katz replied. "That's not our job, anyway.''

"We'd better damn well figure out how we can accomplish our job,'' Manning commented. The Canadian turned to Karl Hahn. "Is there any way we could jam their radio waves so the mercs won't be able to contact Skrubu?''

"That's difficult to attempt without knowing what sort of radio frequency the enemy uses,'' the German electronics expert answered. "Besides, we don't know if Skrubu and Kingston have some sort of hourly radio check.''

"We may have to take that risk if we can't gather more information,'' Katz mused. "That means recon.''

"What about recon *within* the camp?'' Hahn inquired. "The mercenaries might not know any of the details about the gun battle at the FASA building today, but they're bound to know the fight occurred. If they're a bit short-handed, they might welcome a couple of new recruits."

"Just stroll into the camp and ask to join?" Van Schooer glared at Hahn. "You can't be serious, Mr. Kruger."

"I'm serious enough to volunteer for the job," Hahn announced. "If we can manage to get enough details from our captives to conjure up a convincing story, I think I can infiltrate the mercenary camp."

"They might kill you before you can open your mouth," Calvin James warned.

"If a German national approaches and asks to join?" Hahn shrugged. "I doubt that. Of course, they'll kill me in an instant if they suspect anyone is hiding in the bushes watching."

"You're not going in alone," David McCarter announced. "I'll join you. Two men shouldn't seem any more suspicious than one."

"How about three?" James inquired.

"I think that would be stretching credibility a bit too far," Katz stated. "Besides, I don't think an American black would be welcomed by the mercenaries. Neither would a middle-aged man with an artificial arm."

"They might not suspect me," Manning said.

"Kruger and I have already taken the job," McCarter told him. "And I'd feel a lot better knowing our best marksman and explosives expert was covering my arse."

"We won't be able to cover it very well," Manning said. "We won't be able to get close. Even tracking you guys will be pretty tough. The mercs are bound to frisk you and I don't think they'll overlook a transmitter."

"That depends on what sort of transmitter we use," Hahn said. "Are you gentlemen familiar with the infamous bug-in-the-martini device? A wireless microphone that can be concealed inside an olive?"

"That contraption doesn't have much of a range," Katz said with a frown.

"I'm not suggesting we use the actual microphone," Hahn explained, "just a device similar to it that will transmit a low-frequency beep to a receiver. I've got everything I'll need to build such a transistorized beeper. This TV shop is well stocked with the necessary equipment."

"That's ducky," McCarter mused. "But how are we going to carry these olives? I think the mercs would be a bit suspicious if we showed up with a couple of martinis when we ask to join their little private army."

"We'll simply swallow the transmitters," Hahn replied.

"Swallow?" McCarter glared at the German agent. "You've got to be joking?"

"You never heard of a Walkman radio before?" Hahn replied with a shrug. "You and I are going to get to know what it feels like to be one."

"Now, isn't that just bloody wonderful," McCarter muttered.

15

Little of the Republic of South Africa qualifies as jungle. Most of the bush region is located along the coast, and the woodland area, which is home to the majority of South Africa's wild animals, has been converted into well-protected national parks.

Thus, Major Kingston's mercenary base was not a bivouac camp of camouflage-print tents surrounded by a wall of sandbags. The base was a rather unremarkable ranch house in the Acacia savanna, roughly twenty miles south of the Kalahari Gemsbok National Park. The ranch belonged to Lawrence Kotze, a middle-class Afrikaner. Kotze owned one of the largest sheep herds in the republic.

Since wool is a major export of South Africa, Kotze was a respected businessman, the sort of man who would generally be above suspicion. The Kotze ranch was far enough from any towns or cities to allow the rancher to run his spread any way he desired, provided nothing occurred on his property that might evoke the concern of his neighbors. Naturally, everyone in the Acacia savanna knew where the Kotze ranch was located, although few had visited the spread.

David McCarter and Karl Hahn had no trouble getting directions to the Kotze ranch. The British commando drove their Toyota Land Rover while his German companion scanned the area through the lenses of Bushnell binoculars. Hahn did not detect any signs of surveillance equipment or enemy scouts.

Yellow protea flowers seemed to shine in the afternoon sun. Orange and black buttercups—slightly larger than the yellow buttercups familiar to most Americans and Europeans—dotted the ground on either side of the dirt road. A beautiful lavendar candelbra flower waved in the breeze above the tops of a cluster of milkweed. Two springbok antelope warily watched the jeep from a safe distance.

"We ought to be approaching the ranch pretty soon," McCarter commented. "Can you see anything to suggest we're getting close?"

"Not yet," Hahn replied as he lowered the field glasses. "Don't worry. Everyone told us this road leads directly to Kotze's property. The mercenaries will probably know we're coming before we spot their base, anyway. Even if they don't have heat-or sound-activated sensors, a lookout with a powerful telescope would see us approach long before we'd see the ranch."

"I hope those radioactive pills we swallowed are working," McCarter muttered.

"They're not radioactive," the German assured him. "The transmitters are powered by a tiny quartz crystal. The capsules were operating fine before we left, so there's nothing to worry about."

"What if the batteries leak?" McCarter asked.

"They won't leak," Hahn replied. "Besides, you'll pass the capsule when you have your first healthy bowel movement. Don't worry. It won't be inside you long enough to do any harm."

"I bet they used to say the same thing about asbestos," the Briton said with a snort.

He drove the jeep over the summit of a knoll and suddenly the Kotze ranch appeared before them. A barbed-wire fence surrounded the property, which extended beyond their range of vision. Dozens of sheep grazed in the fields of carefully cultivated grass. Three jeeps were parked near the herd. Every vehicle was full of white men and one black African, all armed with FAL or H&K G-3 automatic rifles.

Four more men were stationed by a gate. They were also well armed. One man carried an American-made CAR-15 while the other three held R-4 rifles. The R-4 was manufactured in South Africa and combined the best features of the Russian Kalashnikov and Israeli Galil. The weaponry was strictly full-auto military equipment.

"Stoppen!" a voice shouted as gunmen swung their rifles toward the advancing Land Rover. Others repeated the order in English, German and French, but the muzzles of their weapons spoke a language only an idiot would fail to understand.

McCarter immediately stepped on the brake. The Toyota Land Rover came to a full halt. The gunmen did not alter the aim of their weapons as McCarter and Hahn raised their hands.

"Better save your firepower," the Briton shouted. "The way things were earlier today, we might bloody well need it!"

A collective murmur rippled through the mercenaries. A large man with a barrel chest abruptly ordered the others to shut up.

"You blokes listen to me and you'd best be listenin' good," the group leader warned McCarter and Hahn. His voice contained a firm commanding quality, flavored by a thick Dublin accent. "I want you both to get outta that jeep. Keep your hands high and if you even think 'bout reachin' for a weapon my lads will shoot more holes in you than a limey sailor's got crab lice."

"Oh, God," McCarter muttered. "Just what I needed. A Brit-hating Irishman."

"Is there any other kind?" Hahn remarked as he stepped from the Land Rover.

The big Irishman and two of his comrades approached the Phoenix Force pair. The other gunmen remained behind the wire, weapons held ready.

"Our guns are in the jeep," Karl Hahn began. "We're not stupid enough to try..."

"Shut up," the Irishman snapped. "Before we carry this conversation any further, I want you two stripped down until you're buck-arse naked."

"Things have been a bit slow, eh?" McCarter said dryly.

"Don't get smart with me, you limey shithead," the Irish gunman growled. "Just do what I tell you before my natural instincts make me squeeze the trigger of my ruddy gun."

"Just don't try to squeeze *my* trigger, mate," McCarter commented as he unbuttoned his trousers.

A number of the mercenaries chuckled at the Briton's remark. The Irishman was not amused, but he chose to ignore McCarter's statement. The two Phoenix Force commandos obeyed instructions and removed their clothing. McCarter folded his hands over his crotch, but Hahn raised his arms.

"You bashful, limey?" the Irishman sneered.

"Didn't want to make you jealous, mate," McCarter replied.

"Look," Hahn said quickly, worried that the Briton's sharp tongue might get them killed. "We're certainly not armed now. If you gentlemen will relax, we'll be happy to explain...."

"Search their clothes," the Irishman told his men. "Make certain they don't have any weapons or listening devices hidden away. Then check the jeep."

"*Oui*, Sergeant O'Brian," one of the mercs replied.

"While the lads are checkin' out your stuff," O'Brian began, "you fellas can tell me your story. And it best be pretty good."

"You'd better listen to us before you start shooting," Hahn warned. "My name is Karl Hahn and this is David McCarter."

"That is not what these passports say," a French merc declared, searching through the confiscated clothing. "According to these your names are Kruger and Nelson. *Oui?*"

"The passports are under false names," McCarter replied. "How often do you chaps use your real names when traveling in a foreign country seeking work?"

"They've got submachine guns and pistols in the jeep," another mercenary announced. "What sort of work are you guys lookin' for?"

"We're in the same profession as you fellows," Hahn stated. "Soldiers of fortune. Guns for hire. Sergeant Goodman had contacted us earlier today to participate in a strike carried out against some antiapartheid group. Then he decided he'd better not take us along until Major Kingston had a chance to interview us and officially recruit us into your unit."

"Too bad for Goodman he didn't bring us along," McCarter added. "Might have saved a few lives."

"What do you mean?" O'Brian demanded.

"Word must come out here pretty slow," Hahn commented. "The attack on the antiapartheid headquarters was a disaster, Goodman and every man in his group were killed in the battle."

"Merde alors," the French merc gasped.

"Hold on, mates," O'Brian told his men. "All we've got is their word on that. Not very convincing evidence in my opinion."

"Then turn on a bloody radio and listen to the news," McCarter invited. "They've been talking about it on the radio for the past hour. Heard it on our way here."

"What do you fellas want?" O'Brian asked suspiciously.

"We had planned to join you blokes," McCarter replied. "Don't know for certain what you've got planned or what Major Kingston is up to, but it's the only game in town. Goodman didn't give us any details, but he said the job paid a lot and that's good enough for us."

"They are not carrying any hidden microphones," the Frenchman announced. "Or anything else suspicious. Perhaps they tell the truth."

"Haven't found anything unusual about the jeep," another merc added. "Of course, I'll need more time to take this sucker apart to be sure."

"Do it," O'Brian ordered. "Give them back their clothes, Marteau. You two get dressed. You're comin' with us to see Captain Dietrich."

"Who's Dietrich?" Hahn inquired.

"Kingston's XO, mate," O'Brian explained. "He's in charge while the old man's away. Dietrich is a kraut, too, so you should have a lot to talk about. He'll also be able to figure out if you're really from Germany or just a kraut-speaking South African tryin' to give us a bullshit story. We've got a few limeys in our bunch, too. They'll test you as well, Brit. If either one or both of you are coppers, you'd do well just to admit it now. Be a lot easier on you if'n we just shot you outright."

"You're so considerate," McCarter commented as he pulled on his trousers. "But let's go see Dietrich anyway. Maybe, if you're a good boy, he'll let you pick some potatoes, O'Brian."

"I ought to shoot you right now, Brit," the Irishman growled, aiming his rifle at McCarter's belly.

"Shooting unarmed men a specialty of yours, O'Brian?" McCarter inquired. "Bet you were trained by the IRA. Would it be easier if I turned my back on you, mate?"

"Fuckin' bastard," O'Brian snarled as he handed his gun to Marteau. "I'm going to give you a proper thrashin', limey."

"Sergeant," Marteau began. "Perhaps you should not..."

"Shut up, frog," the Irishman snapped. "I won't kill the Brit. Just knock out a few teeth and maybe break a rib or two."

"You plan to talk me to death or use your fists, O'Brian?" McCarter inquired as he finished tying his bootlaces.

The Irishman charged. He feinted a right cross and swiftly swung a left at McCarter's head. The British warrior dodged the fist and swung a short right to O'Brian's kidney. He followed with a fast left hook to the Irishman's solar plexus and a right cross to his opponent's jaw. O'Brian staggered from the punches, but did not fall.

McCarter kept after his opponent. His left shot out twice, hitting O'Brian in the breastbone and on the point of the jaw. The Irishman's head bounced, but he accepted the punishment and suddenly swung a left hook to the side of McCarter's head. The blow spun McCarter around.

Then McCarter's leg snaked out, slamming a side kick to O'Brian's gut. The Irishman gasped and stumbled. McCarter closed in fast. He chopped the sides of his hands across both of O'Brian's forearms and rapidly swung a left to the Irishman's jaw, followed by a solid uppercut. O'Brian's head danced from the blows and dropped into position to receive a hard elbow smash full in the mouth.

O'Brian weaved on unsteady legs. Blood poured from his split lips and bloodied gums where his front teeth used to be. The Irishman shook his head to clear it and suddenly launched a kick for the Briton's groin. McCarter parried the kick with a heel of the palm. O'Brian swung a left hook, but his wrist met McCarter's right forearm. The Briton jabbed a left to his opponent's chin and followed with a hard right cross. The Irishman fell to one knee. He tried to rise and dropped abruptly to all fours, blood spewing from his open mouth.

"I think you've had enough, mate," McCarter commented as he walked away from his vanquished opponent. "Can we go see Dietrich now?"

"WHAT THE HELL was that nonsense about?" Karl Hahn whispered to McCarter as the two men sat in the back of a jeep driven by one of the mercs. Another vehicle loaded with four gunmen followed behind them.

"What nonsense?" the Briton asked softly, taking a Player's cigarette from its pack. "You mean that donnybrook with O'Brian?"

"What were you trying to prove, damn it?" the German agent growled. Hahn had been assigned to numerous undercover missions in the past, and one of the golden rules of survival is that one never antagonizes individuals of a group one is trying to infiltrate.

"I'll explain later," McCarter promised.

The Briton could not blame Hahn for being upset with his behavior. The BND agent was accustomed to intelligence operations that took weeks or months to gradually gain intelligence by getting the enemy to either trust the infiltrator or take him or her for granted. This was sound and logical procedure. In most operations this was the best way to handle an undercover mission.

However, Phoenix Force was fighting against the clock. Time did not make standard intel techniques acceptable. McCarter's behavior had seemed rash and foolhardy, which was exactly the impression he wanted to give the mercenaries. A fellow who could be goaded into a fistfight with a larger opponent would be regarded as bold, cocky and reckless. This was exactly opposite to the behavior a professional espionage agent would display if he planned to infiltrate the mercenaries.

The jeeps approached a large ranch house. Three mercs lounging about on the front porch snapped to attention when they saw the vehicle. One man quickly entered the house while the other two held their rifles at port arms and stood at either side of the door. Moments later, a stocky figure stepped onto the porch. The man's face was wedge-shaped with small eyes, a compact mouth and a blunt nose. It seemed as if all his features had been pinched together.

"So, our visitors have arrived," he remarked, shoving his fists into his wide hips. "I am Captain Dietrich. You wish to speak with me, *ja*?"

"Ja, mein Herr," Karl Hahn announced as he climbed from the jeep. *"Ich bin Karl Hahn und das ist David McCarter."*

"Don't be rude, Herr Hahn," Dietrich said. "Speak English for the sake of the others. On the radio, Corporal Marteau told me you both speak English. In fact, he said McCarter is an Englishman. One with a sharp tongue and a short temper at that."

"Nobody's perfect, Captain," McCarter declared.

"We are not concerned with perfection," Dietrich stated. "You claim Sergeant Goodman planned to enlist you into our unit?"

"That's correct," Hahn confirmed. "Goodman would have brought us, but he and the men under his command were killed during an assault on an antiapartheid base."

"This news is on the radio, Herr Hahn. At least, they claim all involved in the attack were killed. I wonder why Goodman gave you directions to come here, although he did not trust you enough to take you on the raid?"

"Unfortunately, Goodman is dead and can't answer that question. I know he was concerned about the mission. Goodman had run a recon of the site and discovered it was better defended than he had previously believed. Still, he didn't want to return without trying to accomplish something. He didn't want to admit he backed down because of a 'bunch'a niggers,' I think he called them."

"That sounds like Goodman," Dietrich said. "But I am not convinced we can trust you two. We'll have to question you both. If we decide to let you join, then you'll get to live. Otherwise, we will not be able to risk keeping you alive. *Verstehen?"*

"That's not really very difficult to understand, Captain," Hahn replied. The German agent did not feel terribly confident of his plan now that they were actually inside the mercenary base.

But, he thought, it had seemed like a good idea at the time.

16

Gary Manning watched the wave-length screen of the special radio receiver in the back of the Safari camper parked seven miles from the Kotze ranch. The Canadian was impressed by the contraption. Karl Hahn had revealed his electronic genius when he built the receiver in a matter of hours. The device not only registered the signal from the transmitters swallowed by Hahn and McCarter, it also told Manning whether or not the pair were inside a building or outside.

The transmitters were designed to register body heat, which generally decreased indoors in daytime and increased under the same circumstances after dark. This information was relayed to the receiver and conveyed on the screen. If the "beeper" failed to transmit body heat, this would suggest one or both capsules had been excreted from the host or, more likely, especially if both signals registered the same, the host was dead.

"Has the situation changed yet?" Yakov Katzenelenbogen inquired as he poured himself a cup of coffee.

"Not yet," Manning replied. "They're still inside some sort of large building, unless I'm misreading this screen. You ought to get some more sleep, Yakov. I'll wake you if anything happens."

"I don't feel much like sleeping," Katz said. "And remember to call me Wallburg. Oktoba and Whitney are in the other camper, and either one of them might pay us an unexpected visit at any moment."

"Yeah," Manning said, sighing. "These cover names can be a pain in the ass. What I couldn't understand was why you suggested Karl and David should use their real names when they met with the mercenaries."

"The mercs are going to interrogate them," the Israeli explained. "They'll have the best chance of convincing the enemy that they're telling the truth if they simply tell as much truth as possible. Using their real names is a fundamental truth to begin with."

"I just hope they don't torture David and Karl," Manning remarked, unable to repress a shudder.

"What's the scanner indicate?" Calvin James asked as he climbed out of his bunk. "High body heat suggests stress. Extreme body heat probably means extreme stress. In this case, that would almost certainly be physically induced."

"Body heat level is high," Manning announced. "But not alarming. Karl's registering more stress than David. That figures. Our crazy Englishman is probably bored, waiting for the action to start."

"This waiting is worse than combat," James muttered. "I can't sleep worth a shit. Isn't there something I can do?"

"I've got the radio monitor on and I check the five-twenty frequency every five minutes in case they manage to get to a field radio to contact us," Manning assured him. "There really isn't much else to do until the time limit runs out."

"It's only 2000 hours," Katz stated, glancing at a digital clock above the radio receiver. "Unless the signals suggest our men are being tortured or one of them contacts us by radio, we don't move out until 0400 hours. Sentries tend to be least alert at the first breaking of dawn. They're usually confident the night has passed without incident, and they're eager to be relieved by the next shift."

"And hopefully the rest of the mercs will be sound asleep when we hit the place," James added. "And David and Karl will manage to get out of the line of fire."

"You know there's a fifty-fifty chance the mercs will still be able to radio Skrubu before we can take the place," Manning reminded his teammates.

"We've been over that before," Katz said with a nod. "David and Karl are in a very dangerous position. We can't leave them inside that camp. There isn't time for them to gain the trust and confidence of the enemy. Time is working against us in every direction. If it's humanly possible for our friends to reach a radio and contact us, they'll do it. Otherwise, they may be able to prevent the enemy from contacting Skrubu."

"Or they might be locked in a cell unable to do diddly-shit." James sighed.

"That's possible," Katz admitted. "But the mercs are based at Kotze's ranch house, not a military barracks with a guardhouse and concrete bunkers. I doubt they've got a solid cell with iron bars and stone walls. If the mercs simply lock McCarter and Hahn in a room, I'm certain it won't hold them when the firefight begins."

"Maybe not," Manning said grimly, "providing the mercs don't decide to kill them both the minute the shooting starts."

KARL HAHN WAS TIRED of answering the same questions over and over again. Captain Dietrich had marched the German agent into a small room and had asked Hahn numerous questions about his background, largely to determine if he had actually been born and raised in the Federal Republic of Germany.

With an armed guard stationed at the doorway, Dietrich continued to grill Hahn about his past mercenary experience. Of course, Hahn had never been a soldier of fortune, so he improvised a story about working with the Turkish Gray Wolves.

"The Gray Wolves are right-wing terrorists, aren't they?" Dietrich inquired. "Didn't it bother you to assist such men?"

"I am not political," Hahn said with a shrug. "I was well paid to instruct the Gray Wolves in small arms and technical sabotage."

"Technical sabotage?" Dietrich raised his eyebrows.

"How to foul up computers, short-circuit electrical wiring, that sort of thing," Hahn explained. "I studied electronics and computer programming as a foreign exchange student in the United States."

"That explains why you speak English so well," Dietrich mused. "Tell me, were you in Turkey long enough to master the language there as well?"

"*Turkce biliyor musunuz?*" Hahn asked.

"I don't understand Turkish," Dietrich confessed. "But we have a soldier here who was born in Istanbul. He'll have a chat with you later, Hahn."

"Wonderful," Hahn muttered. "I need to practice the language anyway. I've been living in Germany for the past year, so my Turkish is a bit rusty."

"Tell me again how you were contacted by Sergeant Goodman," Dietrich ordered. "Don't forget all the details about Major Kingston's army. I want to hear everything you were told about us."

Hahn wearily repeated his cover story, which was based on tape recordings made during the Phoenix Force interrogation of Goodman. The German BND agent was glad the mercenaries did not use a truth serum and was equally relieved that Dietrich had not resorted to torture. To use torture under such circumstances would not only ruin a possible new recruit, but would damage morale among the troops as well.

"Your story is consistent," Dietrich announced after listening to Hahn repeat his convincing fiction once more. "A few facts aren't correct, but Goodman may have lied to you and he certainly withheld information for security."

"Does that mean you believe me?" the German agent asked with a sigh.

"It means I'm not going to have you shot." The captain smiled as he took a pack of cigarettes from his shirt pocket. "Care for a smoke?"

"No, thanks, I gave it up a while back," Hahn replied. "Well, what are you going to do with me now?"

"Send in Corporal Torba to question you in Turkish to try to determine how well you speak the language and how long you probably spent in the country," Dietrich answered. "Don't count on getting any sleep tonight, Hahn."

"How about letting me use the bathroom?" Hahn inquired.

"One doesn't usually permit a subject to use the bathroom during an interrogation," Dietrich said with a shrug.

"You're running this show, Captain," Hahn remarked. "But don't be surprised if I piss on the floor before the night is through."

"I don't think it'll hurt to allow you to relieve yourself in a more conventional manner," Dietrich decided. He turned to the guard. "Sergeant Agnello, escort Mr. Hahn to the bathroom and stay with him."

"*Si, Capitano.*" Agnello nodded. "Come with me, Hahn."

The sergeant was a small swarthy man with a droopy black mustache. A bandolier of cartridges was draped over his chest, and Agnello resembled a *bandido* in a Pancho Villa movie. The Italian merc gestured toward the door with the barrel of his South African assault rifle. Hahn walked to the exit, Agnello close behind him.

The West German agent stepped into a spacious hall from which virtually all the furniture had been removed. Only a walnut coat tree remained. Paintings had been taken from the walls and replaced by a bulletin board and a map of South Africa. Hahn noticed the hall was deserted except for a black mercenary seated at a field desk, probably in charge of quarters duty.

Hahn glanced up at a wall clock. It was almost 1:30 A.M. At least four more hours before Phoenix Force was scheduled to attack the mercenary base. Four more hours of tiresome questioning in a bare little room with a painfully bright lightbulb burning down from the ceiling.

The crackle of static drew Hahn's attention to an open door. A young blond merc sat before a large communications radio, a headset clamped to his ears and a microphone in his hand. The radio operator spoke into the mike, but Hahn could not hear the man well enough to be certain what language he spoke, let alone what words were uttered.

"Bathroom is in there," Agnello snapped in thickly accented English, waving his R-4 toward a small door at the opposite side of the hall.

"*Danke schön,*" Hahn replied. "Or should I say *grazie*?"

"You don't have to say anything," Agnello said. "I don't listen much anyway."

Hahn entered the bathroom. Agnello stood at the doorway, bracing the door open with a boot, his weapon pointed in Hahn's direction although the muzzle was tilted toward the floor. Hahn opened his trousers and relieved himself, sighing with genuine pleasure as urine splashed the water within the toilet bowl.

"That was a relief," he remarked as he washed his hands in the sink. "If you have to go, Sergeant, I'll be happy to hold the gun on you while you take a leak."

"Hurry up," Agnello ordered, clearly not amused by the German's remark.

Hahn emerged from the bathroom, escorted by the gun-toting sergeant. Captain Dietrich stood by the desk of the charge-of-quarters NCO, examining the man's written instructions. Two figures approached the main hall from a corridor. One of the mercs was a tall man with an FAL rifle slung over his shoulder. The other was shorter, with an olive complexion and a black goatee.

"Ah," Dietrich began, "Corporal Torba has arrived."

A cold shiver bolted up Hahn's spine when he saw Torba's face. The Turkish mercenary was no stranger to Hahn, although Torba was not the man's real name. He was Mohammed Sihir, formerly of the Turkish People's Army. Sihir had been part of a group of TPA fanatics who had joined forces with the German Red Army faction during a terrorist campaign in Munich in 1979. Hahn was familiar with Sihir's past because he had infiltrated the terrorist group that led to the arrest of Sihir and his comrades.

Corporal Torba's eyes widened and his face stiffened with anger. He obviously remembered Karl Hahn as well. Sihir thrust an accusing finger at the West German agent and began shouting in Turkish, warning his comrades that Hahn was a spy.

"Scheisser," Hahn growled as he suddenly leaped to the coat tree.

Sergeant Agnello was taken off guard by this tactic. He swung his R-4 rifle toward Hahn's new position, but he was not quick enough. The German commando had seized the coat tree and swung it at the Italian mercenary. The heavy X-shaped base slammed into the sergeant's rifle, striking the R-4 from the merc's grasp. Hahn thrust the tree like a *bo-jutsu* stave and smashed the base into Agnello's face. The sergeant dropped to the floor, blood pouring from his shattered mouth and jaws.

"Donnerwetter!" Captain Dietrich cried as he fumbled with the button-flap holster on his hip.

The merc commander started to draw his Walther P-38, but Hahn lunged with the coat tree before Dietrich could clear leather. The phallic-shaped top of the tree rammed into Dietrich's chest, knocking the captain backward into the CQ's desk. Dietrich fell into the lap of the startled charge of quarters noncom.

Mohammed Sihir and the other mercenary charged forward. Sihir dragged a Browning automatic from its holster while his companion unslung the FAL rifle from his shoulder. Hahn hurled the coat tree at the pair, tossing it in a low sweep. The walnut shaft of the tree chopped into their shins, and both men tripped and crashed to the floor.

The black merc on CQ duty abruptly shoved Dietrich to the floor and gathered up his rifle. Hahn's right hand slapped the barrel, pinning it to the field desk. Then Hahn's left fist smacked into the black merc's jaw.

Hahn noticed a ballpoint pen roll along the desk. Holding his opponent's rifle to the desk top with his right hand, he grabbed the pen and snapped his wrist as he thrust the point of the pen into the black's man's face. The tip found its intended target, piercing the NCO's left eyeball. The sergeant shrieked as blood squirted from his face. But the noncom's pain was brief as the force of Hahn's thrust drove the pen deep into the eyesocket to plunge into his opponent's brain.

The German warrior altered his grip on the R-4 and turned the weapon toward Sihir and the other mercenary on the floor. The Turk was trying to aim his Browning pistol at Hahn while his comrade pulled back the bolt of his FAL rifle. Hahn triggered the R-4 and three 5.56 mm slugs slammed into Sihir's chest, splintering his sternum and tunneling through his heart and lungs. The Turkish mercenary sprawled lifeless across the floor as the other soldier of misfortune tried to aim his FAL at Hahn. The German continued to trigger his weapon as he swung the R-4 toward the second gunman. Two bullets crashed into the merc's forehead, splitting bone and drilling through the man's brain.

As Captain Dietrich started to rise from the floor, Hahn stepped behind the merc commander and quickly stamped the folding stock of the R-4 into the base of Dietrich's skull. The captain uttered a faint groan and slumped senseless on his belly. Hahn immediately turned his attention on the radio operator in the commo room.

As the horrified radioman grabbed the microphone and pressed the Transmit button, Hahn opened fire with the R-4. A 3-round burst ripped into the radioman's left triceps and the side of his neck. The multiple bullets kicked him from his chair. Hahn rushed into the commo room, seized the cord of the microphone and yanked it from the radio with a single hard pull.

A door at the opposite side of the hall burst open, and two uniformed figures tumbled across the threshold. Hahn turned his rifle toward the pair, but both men fell to the floor. David McCarter emerged from the room and glanced down at the mercs, rubbing a knuckle on his right fist. One of the men moaned and lifted his head. McCarter promptly kicked him in the face and knocked the merc unconscious.

"I take it the shit hit the fan," McCarter remarked as he noticed Karl Hahn was packing a rifle and the hall was littered with still bodies.

"By the shovelful," the German confirmed.

"Oh, well," the Briton said with a shrug, kneeling beside the two mercs he had rendered senseless. McCarter took an M-16 from the limp grasp of one of the men. "I was bloody bored with their goddamn questions anyway."

McCarter snapped the selector switch to full auto as alarmed voices echoed from the corridor. The Briton trained the M-16 in the direction of the voices and as three uniformed shapes rapidly approached, he triggered the assault rifle, squeezing off two rapid 3-round volleys. Two shapes screamed and melted to the floor while the third retreated from view.

"I found the radio," Hahn announced. "It's temporarily out of order."

The German jogged to the unconscious figure of Sergeant Agnello. He kicked the NCO's R-4 rifle across the floor toward McCarter and hastily opened the ammo pouch on Agnello's belt to extract a spare magazine for the weapon. Without warning, the front door opened and two mercenaries approached. Both men were positioned by the doorway, exposing only a portion of their faces and arms as they extended the barrels of their assault rifles.

McCarter's M-16 sprayed the door with 5.56 mm rounds. One merc screamed as he fell, blood bubbling from a wound under his right eye. The other ducked for cover. Karl Hahn scrambled to McCarter's position, and both men moved into the interrogation room where the Briton had been questioned by the two mercs who now lay senseless on the floor.

"I managed to get a spare mag and this ammo belt off Agnello's chest," Hahn announced, breathing hard from exertion and stress. "All 5.56 caliber. Same for the R-4 as for the M-16...."

"Glad you got your shopping done," McCarter commented. "But we're not in the best position for a firefight. The bastards can hit us from at least two sides. The only advantage about this room is the fact there isn't a window they can shoot through from the outside. Won't take too long for them to simply decide to blast the wall with a bit of explosives to *make* a bloody window."

"What strategy do you suggest?" Hahn asked, shoving the spare mag for his R-4 into a pocket.

"I suggest we try to stay alive as long as we can and kill as many of the enemy as as possible before they kill us," the British warrior answered.

17

The sound of automatic fire was detected by a rifle-microphone among the surveillance gear used by the Phoenix Force stake-out crew. A long-range microphone with several aluminum tubes and a powerful amplifier, the rifle-mike is a simple yet highly efficient device, and it immediately informed Katz, Manning and James that their partners were in trouble.

"Alert Whitney and Oktoba to follow our lead," Katz announced as he gathered up his Uzi submachine gun. "Tell them to be ready for action because we're moving on the Kotze ranch *immediately*."

"Right," James replied, switching on a walkie-talkie to contact the two BSS agents in the other camper.

"I'll get topside and strap myself in," Gary Manning told his partners. The Canadian held an FN FAL rifle with a Starlite night scope mounted to the frame.

"Make sure you're strapped down firmly," Katz warned. "We're going to burn rubber and I don't want you falling off."

"Oktoba and Whitney are ready to roll," Calvin James declared, grabbing his M-16 rifle with a grenade launcher attached to the barrel.

"Good," Katz said with a nod. "Let's go do our job."

Moments later, James drove the camper straight for the Kotze ranch. His M-16 was propped on the seat beside him. Katz sat in the passenger seat, his Uzi in his left hand and an M-79 grenade launcher positioned at his feet.

Gary Manning rode on the roof of the camper. The Canadian commando was held fast by an X-shaped harness similar to a parachute rig. The straps were buckled at the middle of Manning's back as he lay on his belly, peering through the Starlite night scope mounted on his rifle.

The camper rapidly approached the fences surrounding the Kotze ranch. Half a dozen mercenaries stationed at the gate heard the vehicle, and four men aimed their weapons in the general direction of the camper engine sounds while the other two headed for jeeps to radio headquarters. Neither man suspected that Manning was already watching them through his light-density scanner.

The Canadian marksman squeezed the trigger of his FAL, and a mercenary's head jerked violently as a large portion of his skull exploded. The man collapsed across the field radio he was about to switch on. The other mercs heard the report of Manning's rifle and saw their comrade fall. A split second later, another 7.62 mm missile crashed into the face of the other soldier of fortune who was about to alert his headquarters.

The remaining mercs were uncertain what to do. The approaching vehicle did not have its headlights on so it remained a large shadow in the darkness. A poor target at best and the mercs were already being picked off by an enemy marksman. The logical move would ordinarily have been to head for the jeeps for cover or possible flight, but the mystery sniper was obviously watching the vehicles like a nighthawk.

"Hit the bloody dirt, damn it!" Sergeant O'Brian ordered, deciding a prone position was the best cover they could hope for under the circumstances.

"The idiots are bunched together," Calvin James remarked, gazing through night-view binoculars. The infrared lenses allowed him to see the mercenaries clearly despite the darkness. "They're hugging the ground, but they're still huddled together."

"Must have been a while since they went into combat against anyone who shoots back," Yakov Katzenelenbogen remarked as he gathered up the M-79. "They're reacting out of fear instead of training. We caught them off guard and they're still confused, but it won't take them long to realize they should spread out."

"They aren't going to have enough time," James announced as he stepped on the brake. "We're within range, Yakov."

James opened the door on the driver's side of the cab. Both men aimed their weapons at the enemy position. Katz braced the M-79 "blooper" across his prosthesis, the buttstock jammed in his hip, while James elevated the barrel of his assault rifle and inserted a finger in the trigger guard of the M-203 attachment.

Both men fired their grenade launchers. Two 40 mm projectiles loaded with heavy explosives sailed into the night sky and descended on the enemy position. The grenades erupted with one monstrous voice. The explosion blasted the mercenaries into mangled, bloodied chunks clad in tattered rags. One of the jeeps was bowled over by the blast and crashed into the side of another vehicle.

"Leopard Two, this is Leopard One," Katz spoke into a walkie-talkie. "Do you read me? Over."

"Leopard Two, here," Whitney's voice replied from the transceiver. The South African BSS agent sounded more British than David McCarter. "You chaps had a bit of action, I notice. Over."

"It's finished now," Katz assured him. "Continue to advance, Leopard Two. Contact Leopard Three and Four and tell them to stand by, but stay alert. Some of the quarry will probably scatter when things heat up. Can't have any getting away. Over."

"Affirmative," Whitney assured him.

"Very good, Leopard Two," Katz said. "Over and out."

James slid behind the wheel and Katz resumed his seat next to the black man. The camper rolled forward, entering the Kotze ranch through a large hole in the fence the explosion had provided. The tires struck a bump and James wondered if the obstruction was a dead body.

As the camper raced toward the ranch house, sounds of gunfire continued to register on the rifle-microphone. This meant McCarter and Hahn were still in trouble, but it also meant they were still alive. The sound of full-auto weapons roared from the speakers within the camper until Gary Manning switched it off with a remote-control box. The noise was a dangerous distraction they could not afford as they moved deeper into enemy territory.

Two jeeps suddenly bolted toward the invading camper. Both enemy vehicles were equipped with Swiss-made MG710-2 light machine guns, mounted at the rear of each jeep. Mercenary killers manned the chatter guns, firing twin volleys of 7.62 mm fury at the Phoenix Force camper. The jeeps steered a wide arc around the other vehicle, planning to get the camper in a deadly cross fire.

Manning aimed his FN FAL carefully, peering through the Starlite scope until he found the machine gunner of one of the enemy jeeps. The Canadian squeezed off a 3-round burst. The gunman's head snapped back from the impact of a trio of high-velocity slugs. His body followed and the merc toppled over the rear of the speeding vehicle.

The Canadian marksman swung his rifle toward the other jeep, but the second vehicle had swung a wide circle to the west. Manning could not maneuver his FAL well enough to track the jeep because the harness that held him to the camper roof also inhibited movement.

A salvo of full-auto rounds smashed into the camper, drilling a column of holes in the body. One slug struck the cab, burying itself in the metal skin of the doorjamb inches from James's head.

Gary Manning reached for a hand grenade on his belt, pinning the FAL rifle under his elbows as he pulled the pin from an M-26 blaster. Throwing the grenade was an awkward task, lying on his belly and trying to hurl the mini-bomb over his shoulder at an opponent twenty feet away. Manning clenched his teeth and swung his arm forcibly. The grenade sailed from his hand and whistled toward the enemy jeep.

The M-26 fell short of its target, landing in front of the mercenary vehicle. However, the jeep kept coming and drove right over the grenade as it exploded. Men and machine were ripped apart and thrown ten feet in the sky.

The driver of the first jeep decided it was unhealthy to get too close to the camper. Especially since his machine gunner had been shot out of the saddle. The driver headed behind the Phoenix Force vehicle and brought his jeep to a dead stop. He quickly climbed from the seat and hurried to the MG710-2. Perhaps he could disable the invader by hitting the camper from the rear.

Suddenly, he heard the engine of another vehicle. The merc turned to see the second camper roar on the scene. He started to swing the machine gun around, but the torrent of 5.56 copper-jacketed hornets crashed into his chest and he slumped across the Swiss blast machine.

"By Jove!" Captain Whitney exclaimed as he pulled his head, shoulders and R-4 rifle through the window. "I got the blighter. Charge on, Sergeant Major. Into the Valley of Death and all that."

"Captain," Sergeant Major Oktoba said dryly, steering the camper around the enemy jeep, "I hope you'll bear in mind that the charge of the Light Brigade was not a great victory."

"Whatever do you mean, Sergeant Major?" Whitney asked, genuinely confused.

"Never mind, sir," Oktoba said, sighing. "But please don't shout 'tallyho.' I don't think I can drive and throw up at the same time."

DAVID MCCARTER AND Karl Hahn did their best to defend their position. The commandos were attacked from the corridor and the front of the hall, but the mercenaries quickly learned that the Phoenix Force warriors were far from sitting ducks. The pair fired their weapons with deadly accuracy and professional cunning. Hahn and McCarter covered each other's moves and conserved ammo as best they could under the circumstances.

The gunmen in the corridor suddenly opened up with a mighty salvo of full-auto fire. McCarter guessed at least three weapons were being fired simultaneously.

"They're pinning us down," McCarter declared. "That means the bastards are going to hit us from a different direction."

The Briton's prediction was one hundred percent accurate. Mercenaries at the front entrance lobbed two grenades at the Phoenix Force pair. McCarter slammed the door and the grenades pounded the panels and bounced into the hall. The Briton and the German dived to the floor and covered their heads as a powerful explosion roared in the hall. The blast tore the door off its hinges and shook plaster loose from the walls.

"Are you all right?" McCarter asked his German friend as he rose from the floor and shook plaster dust from his hair.

"So far," Hahn replied. "But I don't think that condition will last much..."

Two mercenaries appeared at the doorway, rifle barrels thrust through the gap. McCarter triggered his M-16, but the weapon did not respond. The Briton's rifle had jammed.

Hahn's R-4 spit fire. A merc hurtled back into the hall, his face split open by a trio of bullet holes. The other soldier of fortune fired a hasty volley with his Beretta M-12 subgun. Parabellum rounds splintered wood from the floorboards near Karl Hahn. The German returned fire, burning four 5.56 mm slugs through the chest and throat of his opponent. The merc slumped against the doorjamb, his body convulsing. The spasms ceased as death claimed another recruit.

A new wave of automatic fire thundered from outside the ranch house. Screams mingled with the metallic chatter of submachine guns and the bellow of a twelve gauge. McCarter laughed, an expression of relief rather than amusement.

"Our mates are here," he announced. "I'd know that sound from any other combat team in the whole bloody world!"

Once again, McCarter was correct. Katz, James and Manning had arrived at the ranch house. Most of the mercenaries were too busy trying to handle McCarter and Hahn to even notice the camper. Others assumed it was one of the unit jeeps. Only two mercs realized a new threat had arrived. They aimed their rifles at the Safari vehicle, but Gary Manning cut them down with his sniper rifle before either man could fire a shot.

Manning quickly unbuckled the harness and climbed down from the roof as James brought the camper to a halt. The Canadian opened the back of the trailer and ducked inside long enough to exchange the FAL for a Remington semiautomatic shotgun with a SWAT-style folding stock. Manning quickly slipped into a small backpack that contained five rounds of C-4 and two pounds of CV-38. The Canadian demolitions expert doubted that he would need all the explosive power he carried, but he believed it was better to have extra blasting power and not need it than to need it and not have it.

Yakov Katzenelenbogen emerged from the camper with his Uzi hung from a shoulder strap near his left hip and his SIG-Sauer P-227 autoloader sheathed in a shoulder holster under his right arm. He held the M-79 grenade launcher and raised the thick barrel to fire a 40 mm missile at the ranch house. The grenade hurtled over the roof and crashed to earth, exploding on impact. Columns of thick green smoke spewed from the canister, forming a dense cloud around the disoriented mercenaries.

Calvin James charged forward with his M-16 ready for action. The black commando also carried his Colt Commander in shoulder leather and the Jet Aer fighting dagger in a sheath under his right arm.

The mercenaries outside the house were confused and half-blinded by the mysterious fog of green smoke that had suddenly swept over them. They did not realize Katz, James and Manning were attacking them until it was too late. The Uzi and M-16 blasted several mercs, while two terrified enemy soldiers managed to dash from the green mist only to receive two volleys of buckshot from Manning's Remington shotgun. The mercs were thrown six feet by the 12-gauge power punches, their chests crushed by number-four pellets.

Katz and James entered the house while Manning jogged to the rear of the building. McCarter and Hahn saw two familiar figures charge into the hall. Tentacles of green smoke drifted across the threshold as James and Katz entered.

"Gunmen down the corridor!" McCarter shouted.

Yakov Katzenelenbogen immediately fired a short burst of Uzi lead into the narrow hallway. James stepped from behind the Israeli and triggered his M-203 launcher. A 40 mm messenger of destruction rocketed to the end of the corridor and exploded with fearsome force. The powerful concussion grenade shook the building, and mercenaries wailed in agony as they clamped their hands over their eardrum-shattered skulls.

"You two okay?" James asked his British and German partners.

"I could do with a nice cold Coca-Cola," McCarter replied as he scooped up a Beretta submachine gun abandoned by a slain mercenary. "Other than that, we're fine."

"Let's mop up this mess," Katz announced.

The Israeli led the way as they entered the corridor. Dead and disabled mercenaries littered the floor, none of them in any condition to threaten the assault team. Katz pressed his back to the wall as he carefully approached an open doorway.

The Phoenix commander peered into the room. Four wounded mercs were clustered around a long dining table. Two men were unconscious and a third was moaning softly, his head cradled in his arms. The fourth man's left arm had been smashed by two bullets, but he held a .38-caliber Smith & Wesson revolver in his right fist.

Katz triggered his Uzi. Three 9 mm rounds ripped the guy open from jawbone to eyebrow. The merc tumbled backward and fell into the table. A shape moved near the doorway. Katz glanced at the form out of the corner of his eye and tried to dodge the bulky object aimed at his left arm.

A tough mercenary swung a chair overhead. He had abandoned his weapon after the concussion blast had wrecked his left eardrum, but the soldier of fortune still had some fight left. He was not quick enough to strike Katz before the Israeli could move, but a chair leg hit Katz's Uzi hard enough to knock the subgun from his hand.

The chair continued to descend, one leg snapping off when it struck the floor. Katz quickly slashed the steel talons at the end of his prosthetic right arm, raking the points across the man's biceps. Cloth ripped and skin split as the metal claws sunk into muscle.

The mercenary screamed and released the chair. Katz's fist smashed into his opponent's jaw. The merc started to stagger, and the Israeli drove a steel uppercut to the man's stomach, punching with the hard curve of his hook. The man doubled up with a gasp, and Katz slugged his fist into the side of his opponent's skull. The merc dropped to the floor, out cold.

"Shit, Yakov," James remarked. "You didn't leave much for us to do."

"There are still more rooms to check," the Phoenix Force commander replied.

The fighting unit continued down the corridor. They encountered several rooms, but none was occupied. Fortunately, the ranch house was only one story high so they did not have to worry about mounting a flight of stairs to hunt down their quarry.

The commandos approached the last room. A lone figure, dressed only in boxer shorts, appeared at the door with a British-made Sterling submachine gun. Katz and James opened fire. Half a dozen 9 mm and 5.56 mm rounds plastered the gunman's torso, tearing his chest apart and hurling him back into the room.

Two mercenaries saw their comrade hit the tile floor of the kitchen. Armed only with pistols, they did not see any logic in trying to take on the mysterious and formidable strike force in the corridor. The pair rushed to a rear exit, yanked open the door and dashed outside.

Gary Manning was waiting for them.

"Freeze!" the Canadian ordered as he dropped to one knee and pointed the Remington shotgun at the mercenaries.

One of the gunmen whirled and tried to aim his pistol at the voice. Manning's shotgun bellowed. A burst of double-O-buckshot smashed into the man's chest. Lethal pellets shredded the merc's heart and lungs as the force propelled his body backward. His corpse tumbled across the ground like a blood-laced tumbleweed.

The other mercenary tossed down his pistol and raised his hands in surrender. The Canadian ordered him to lie on the ground spread-eagle. The merc did not seem to understand so Manning repeated the order in French. A vigorous nod confirmed that the man got the point. He quickly dropped on his belly and stretched out his arms and legs.

A burst of automatic fire behind Manning drew the Canadian's attention. He whirled, pivoting on his knee and swinging the Remington toward the gunshots. Sergeant Major Oktoba, an R-4 rifle in his fists, stood over a dead mercenary. A curl of smoke rose from the barrel of the gun.

"Appears we arrived too late to participate in most of the action," Oktoba commented.

"Your timing was perfect as far as I'm concerned, Sergeant Major," Manning assured him, uttering a deep sigh of relief.

18

Phoenix Force sorted out their vanquished enemies, finding the living among the dead. The latter far outnumbered the former and many survivors were severely wounded. Calvin James tended to the injured while Yakov Katzenelenbogen told Captain Whitney to contact Leopard Three and Four. These consisted of two units of Bureau of Security Services agents and veterans of the Reconnaissance Commandos.

The Recces, as they are often referred to in South Africa, are among the toughest fighting men in the world. It is not surprising that South Africa would have superb commandos since the term once referred to the elite shock troops of the Boers, famed for their hit-and-run tactics against the British during the Boer War. The Recces specialized in missions behind enemy lines, generally acquiring data about SWAPO terrorists in Angola.

Honed by a forty-two-week training program, the Recces can live off the land in the hostile environment of the deserts of South African countries. They are qualified in parachute, small arms, hand-to-hand combat and even underwater warfare. The Recces have been compared to the SAS, the Green Berets and other elite fighting forces.

The Recces had been called in to assist the BSS in order to deal with any mercenaries who might have escaped the battle with Phoenix Force. Leopard Three and Leopard Four drove in a huge circle around the Kotze ranch area. Katz instructed Captain Whitney to inform the two units to move in. If they encountered any of Major Kingston's hired killers, or anyone else for that matter, they were to take him captive if possible. If they had to kill him, that was okay, too.

Fate seemed to smile on Phoenix Force at last. They had successfully located and taken a major enemy base. Perhaps the most encouraging news was that Captain Dietrich, second in command of Kingston's private army, had survived the carnage. Dietrich had been left unconscious by the CQ desk at the beginning of the battle. Shielded by the flimsy furniture and a wall, the captain had suffered from some shrapnel wounds in both legs and a throbbing headache.

"What do you want to do with this son of a bitch?" David McCarter inquired as he dragged Dietrich into the center of the hall.

"We'll want to question him, of course," Katz replied. "Get a chair from the dining room and something to strap him down."

"Was ist das scheisser?" Dietrich said through clenched teeth. "I demand medical attention."

"You will get whatever we decide to give you," Katz replied in curt German. "That includes death, mutilation and castration. So shut up until we tell you otherwise."

"I think we can use belts from some of the dead men to strap Dietrich to the chair," Karl Hahn suggested.

"Sounds fine," Katz confirmed. "Tell Mr. Walker to save some morphine in case Captain Dietrich decides to cooperate. Otherwise, he'll probably have to use scopolamine on the captain."

"Scopolamine?" Dietrich rasped. "Who are you people?"

"We represent the interests of the free world in general and the United States in particular," Katz explained. "Now, there's been a rash of rotten little groups of fanatics and opportunists kidnapping Americans for various reasons. Usually for some sort of ransom or as pawns for negotiation. That trend has got to stop. Some people are going to suffer for that sort of behavior and you're going to be one of them—unless you cooperate, Captain.''

"I don't know what you're talking about," Dietrich declared.

"I'm talking about Senator Finley and Reverend Lincoln," the Phoenix Force commander replied. "One way or the other, you're going to tell us where they are."

"I don't know where they are," the captain insisted.

"Kingston knows," Katz said with a shrug, taking a pack of Camels from his shirt. "And I don't think Kingston is stupid enough to trust Tai Skrubu to the extent that he wouldn't tell you the location of Skrubu's base. Otherwise, Skrubu could simply kill Kingston and not have to worry about paying you chaps because you wouldn't know where to find him—nor be in a position to tell the South African authorities where to find him. Those Recce commandos are excellent trackers. I doubt if Skrubu could get far enough away fast enough to escape them if you talked to the authorities."

"I don't know anything about a kidnapping," Dietrich said.

"That's unfortunate," Katz said, shaking his head. "This could either be a new beginning for you, or the end."

"Beginning?" The captain frowned. "You're playing carrot and stick, eh? I believe the English expression is 'fuck you.'"

"Such language," Katz said. "Of course, the carrot is real and so is the stick."

McCarter returned with a chair, and Hahn had collected several belts. They hastily hauled Dietrich from the floor and placed him in the chair. Katz calmly puffed a cigarette as he continued.

"I'm going to be honest with you, Captain," the Israeli announced. "Goodman and Akerhune don't know where Skrubu is holding Finley and Lincoln. I doubt that any of your other flunkies know much more than they did. However, I believe *you* know all about it, Dietrich. For that reason, we'll be very nasty with you if you don't talk.''

"I'd enjoy working you over, Dietrich," Hahn stated. "You and I are both Germans, but you're a personification of the neo-Nazi stereotype that people still associate with us. You're a gangster in a uniform and a murderer with a military rank. You remind me of a nightmare that happened before I was born, a nightmare that still haunts Germany. This frustrates me and I would like to take out my frustration on you.''

"I'm no Nazi, damn it!" Dietrich snapped.

"You'll be good practice for when I get my hands on one," Hahn said with a cruel smile.

"Take it easy, Kruger," Katz told Hahn. "I'll let you practice on Dietrich if he doesn't respond to the carrot. You see, Captain, we want to find that base. We want Lincoln and Finley—as well as Skrubu's head—more than we want you.''

"You're offering me a deal?" Dietrich asked hopefully.

"I don't like making deals with scum like you," Katz replied. "But that's exactly what I'm offering. Sometimes we have to let little fish go in order to catch a big one."

"What will you give me?" Dietrich wanted to know. "Amnesty?"

"I can't promise that," Katz replied. "However, if you help us I'm positive you won't be charged with conspiracy to kidnap and murder. That still leaves espionage against the Republic of South Africa. If you testify as a state's witness against the others, I think they'll probably drop that charge as well and simply deport you.''

Dietrich nodded slowly. After a couple of minutes of silence, he said, "Very well. Tai Skrubu is holed up at an abandoned copper mine in the Orange Free State. I'll mark it for you on the map.''

"Is the mine located near a lake or river?" Katz asked.

"Not really," Dietrich answered. "It's in a valley. More like a big gorge. Rock walls on all sides. Two main tunnels and a number of caves. Lincoln and Finley are kept in one of the caves. It was converted into a cell by putting in some iron bars.''

Katz nodded. Everything Dietrich said agreed with what Goodman and Akerhune had told them under the influence of scopolamine.

''What's the security like?'' Hahn asked.

''You'll have a problem getting the Americans out alive,'' Dietrich warned. ''All Skrubu's men need to do is toss a grenade into the cave and they'll kill the prisoners and the sentry who's in there with them. You also have to give a password in Swahili before entering the cave or the guard will shoot them. The passwords are changed every day. I can't help you with that.''

''How large is the opposition?'' Katz asked.

''Skrubu has at least thirty Congolese troops. Loyalists from his days as president of Mardaraja. The worst of the lot is his personal bodyguard. Some sort of Bantu warrior sect. Major Kingston is probably still there as well. He's got about ten mercs with him. He picked the best fighting men in our unit.''

''What about security devices?'' Hahn inquired. ''Camera systems, sound detectors, robot trap-guns, anything like that?''

''Skrubu isn't much for high-tech,'' Dietrich replied. ''I don't think he has anything like that, but don't put it past him. Skrubu is shrewd. The cheeky bastard is trying to auction off South Africa to the highest bidder.''

''What?'' Katz glared at him. ''Is this a joke?''

''Sounded ridiculous to me, too,'' Dietrich admitted. ''But that's why he had us abduct Lincoln and Finley in the first place. Part of a scheme to start a revolution in South Africa. Then whoever paid Skrubu, gets to claim what's left of the country.''

''Skrubu isn't shrewd,'' Katz commented. ''He's desperate and possibly insane.''

"Crazy or not," Dietrich began, "Skrubu got bidders. SWAPO was interested, of course, but they couldn't come up with enough money. Libya was contacted, but I don't think Kaddafi trusts Skrubu after that embassy business last year. Zimbabwe was hot for the property, too. There was a Cuban at the base the other day. I think he might have sealed the deal."

"My God," Katz whispered. "Are you certain the Cubans actually sent someone? Was he an officer? Field grade?"

"I think he was supposed to be a lieutenant colonel stationed in Angola," Dietrich said with a shrug. "Is it really that important?"

"The Cubans are acting for the Soviets in Africa," Katz stated. "Moscow wants South Africa, but they'd never agree to something this risky unless they were sure they could destroy any evidence linking them to an attempted revolution. They damn sure don't want to be connected to kidnapping a U.S. senator and a black American evangelist. Why should Moscow pay Skrubu? If the revolution succeeds, the Communists would probably move in anyway. If it fails, it would just be an embarrassment."

"Then why did the Cuban even agree to meet with Skrubu?" Hahn wondered aloud.

"Perhaps to pinpoint where Skrubu's headquarters is," the Phoenix Force commander replied. "So they can destroy it along with everyone there, especially Finley and Lincoln."

"The Cuban was blindfolded and they drove him all the way from the Mozambique border to the site," Dietrich stated. "How could he tell them where the base is?"

"A radio homing device carried in by the Cuban and left at the base would be all they'd need," Hahn declared.

"*Nein.*" Dietrich shook his head. "The Cuban was subjected to a skin search and he was forced to put on different clothing to be certain he did not have a radio transmitter disguised as a button or whatever. It would be impossible for him to carry such a device undetected.''

   ''Unless he swallowed it,'' Hahn said grimly.

19

"The Recces stopped four escaping mercenaries fleeing from the Kotze ranch," Captain Whitney reported to Katz. "Three of the idiots tried to put up a fight. Naturally, that means they only took one merc alive."

"So long as none of them got away," Katz replied, feeding a fresh magazine into his Uzi subgun. "Even if one did, it won't make much difference now. We'll have to hit Skrubu's base as soon as transportation can be arranged. Any stray merc won't have time to reach the enemy headquarters, even if he knows where it is."

"You really think it's wise to rush into this?" the BSS officer inquired.

"We don't have any choice," Katz told him. "The Communists will attack Skrubu's base as soon as possible. If we don't get there first, Lincoln and Finley are as good as dead."

"You can't be certain of that," Whitney insisted.

"We've crossed swords with the KGB on more than one occasion," the Phoenix Force commander declared. "I understand a little about how the Kremlin operates. I'm not infallible, but I've got a pretty good record for guessing how the Reds will react to situations. I think they'll attack as soon as they can zero in on the homing signal."

"You can't know that this Cuban colonel was carrying a capsule transmitter in his gut and . . . defecated it into a latrine at Skrubu's base," Whitney said. "Just because Mr. Kruger used the tactic doesn't mean . . ."

"The Communists aren't less clever than we are," Katz told him. "If anything, they would probably have a more sophisticated radio capsule than Kruger could come up with at your safe house. True, I might be jumping to conclusions. But we're going to raid Skrubu's base. Even if I'm wrong about the Cubans and the Russians, there can be no doubt that Lincoln and Finley are in extreme danger."

"I know," Whitney said, nodding. "And it is as important to us South Africans that those two be rescued as it is to you Americans."

"Slight change in the Recce report, gentlemen," Sergeant Major Oktoba announced as he approached the pair. "The mercenary they captured alive turned out to be none other than Lawrence Kotze, the Afrikaner rancher who was giving aid and comfort to the enemy."

"I wonder what reason he'll give for conspiring against his own country," Captain Whitney growled.

"Probably claim some sort of political convictions about trying to liberate the oppressed," Katz remarked. "But the real reason is probably M-O-N-E-Y. A traitor like Kotze is the worst kind of mercenary."

"I've studied this map that Dietrich marked for us," David McCarter announced. "If you blokes can get us an aircraft large enough to carry all five of us, I can fly us to the site of the copper mine before dawn."

"The Recon Commandos arrived in Lufttijger gunships," Whitney stated. "Have you ever flown one before?"

"Can't say as I have," the British ace pilot confessed. "But if it has wings, a rotor blade or a sack of hot air, I can handle it."

"The Recces feel a bit cheated," Sergeant Major Oktoba said with a grin. "They were hoping to see more action tonight. What they got only whetted their appetites. I'm sure they'd like to join you. So would I, for that matter. I've been with you chaps since this thing began and I'd like to be in on the closing act."

"The sergeant major has handled himself pretty well throughout this mission," Gary Manning announced. "He saved my tail tonight."

"Just returning the favor, Mr. Summer," Oktoba assured him. "I might be useful for your final battle. I speak Swahili, Zulu and Xsopho. Virtually all the Recces are white. They're quite good at camouflaging their skin to resemble a black man's from a distance, but nothing looks as much like a black African as a black African. I might come in handy depending on how we decide to take out the sentries and slip into Skrubu's camp."

"All right, Sergeant Major," Katz decided. "You're in. We'll ask for volunteers from the Recces, but they'll have to understand that my team is in charge. They are to take orders from us and do exactly what we say."

"I'm certain you'll have no trouble getting a gunship full of eager volunteers, Mr. Wallburg," Oktoba said.

"Very good," Katz replied. He turned to Whitney. "Captain, you and the BSS and Recces who don't accompany us on the raid will have to take care of the prisoners here. Keep Dietrich separate from the others. Remember, he's a state witness and he's cooperated with us. Keep him healthy."

"You chaps just concentrate on staying healthy yourselves," Whitney urged. "I have a feeling that might not be so easy."

STOYAN KOSTADINOV HAD ACQUIRED a taste for decadent South African wine. The thirty-seven-year-old Bulgarian poured more crimson liquid into a glass as he solemnly gazed up at the clock on the mantel above his fireplace. It was almost 3:00 A.M. Soon, Kostadinov would have to prepare for his mission.

Kostadinov sometimes forgot he was Bulgarian. He had lived in South Africa for more than ten years. Neighbors knew him as Wilhelm Picol, a good-natured Dutch immigrant who operated a one-man air service. Picol was a slightly eccentric pilot who made a living with his battered old Beech airplane. No one suspected he was actually a Communist agent, a mole working for the Bulgarian Secret Service and thus for the Soviet KGB that controlled it.

Like that of most intelligence operatives, Kostadinov's career had been neither exciting nor sinister. He simply gathered information. Much of this had come from open sources—newspapers, magazines, Johannesburg television and verbal opinions of people Kostadinov encountered as a private pilot. Kostadinov's occupation also allowed him to fly over various cities, hamlets, farmlands, mining projects and an occasional military installation.

Kostadinov collected this rather unspectacular intelligence and wrote it in code words, spaced among sentences in innocent-looking letters. Every other month, he left the messages inside the pages of a French translation of the Koran at the public library in Kroonstad. This was possibly the least used book in the place. Another Communist operative would later retrieve the letter and pass it on to the Soviet embassy.

These simple espionage chores seemed harmless to Kostadinov. He did not mind his job. It gave him an excuse to travel all over South Africa. After more than a decade in the country, Kostadinov considered himself to be "an honorary Afrikaner." He liked living in the republic. People had far more rights than Bulgarians in his homeland. Even blacks and coloreds in South Africa were treated better than most Bulgarian citizens, let alone the Turkish minority in Bulgaria.

In the winter of 1984, the Bulgarian government passed a "unity act" that required all citizens of Turkish descent to assume Bulgarian names. Turks who refused to change their names accordingly were arrested and jailed. At least two were shot. Kostadinov noticed there was no great outcry of "violation of human rights" by the U.N. concerning this incident. The Americans and British, who never tired of criticizing South Africa for apartheid, barely noticed what had happened in Bulgaria.

Kostadinov had no desire to return to his homeland. He had hoped to quietly continue his covert operations for the Soviets, providing enough intelligence data to keep the KGB off his back. Then, with a bit of luck and a lot of obscurity, he might be able to live out the rest of his life in South Africa.

However, yesterday, Stoyan Kostadinov had received a visit from three KGB officers attached to the Soviet embassy. A major from Department Eleven, which controls all Bulgarian intelligence operations, personally assigned a new mission to Kostadinov. He was ordered to fly over a small abandoned mine in the Orange Free State and destroy it.

The two lower-ranking agents of the Komitet Gosudarstvennoi Bezopasnosti went to work on Kostadinov's plane. They installed a special radio receiver in the control panel of the old Beech. The box would detect a beeping signal from a transmitter that had been planted at the target site. Two oil drums were attached to the belly of the plane. The Russians explained that the barrels contained a powerful incendiary explosive, something the Soviets had been using against the reactionary bandits in Afghanistan.

But why did the KGB want Kostadinov to bomb an old mine?

"You have been chosen to perform a service for the People's Revolution against imperialism," the major answered. "It is in the interest of our struggle on this continent, Comrade. That is all you need to know."

Kostadinov knew better than to refuse a direct order from the KGB. Suicide had never appealed to the Bulgarian. Kostadinov recalled the grim encounter as he sat alone in his kitchenette, drinking his wine.

"Goddam those *Moskavite* bastards," he said, shaking his head sadly. "I never killed anyone. Why do they want me to do this? KGB enjoy killing people. Why don't those butchers do it themselves?"

Of course, Kostadinov knew the answer. The Russians never did the dirty work if they could use a Cuban, a Bulgarian or even a Ukrainian instead. Kostadinov sighed, accepting the circumstances fate had thrust upon him. He finished his glass of wine.

20

Phoenix Force was behind schedule. The five-man strike team, Sergeant Major Oktoba and a dozen Recon Commandos did not reach the old McClearry copper mine until shortly after daybreak. They had hoped to launch their assault at predawn. There was only a few minutes' difference, yet already the conditions were more difficult.

Sounds of activity within Tai Skrubu's camp warned them that at least some of the enemy force was already awake. The assault unit examined the base through binoculars. Skrubu's people had set up four large tents at the base of the valley. Three deuce-and-a-half trucks and two jeeps were parked nearby. This seemed a bit odd until one noticed a long flat incline had been formed along one wall of the gorge. The mining crew had built this road in order to get equipment in and out of the valley.

The McClearry Mining Company had done a lot of work on the rock walls of the area before the copper petered out. Skrubu had taken advantage of the tunnels and caves that had been dug into the stone by the miners. At least one mine shaft appeared to be a combination supply room and emergency bomb shelter. Caves were apparently used to store food and water, protected from the heat of the African sun. It seemed likely the terrorists had also stored ammunition and explosives in one or more caves.

Locating the one that housed Senator Tom Finley and Reverend Robert Lincoln was not difficult. A sentry was positioned near the mouth of the cave. The sentry, a black man, was dressed in French-style camouflage uniform and a brown beret, which suggested he was probably a Congolese trooper. He was armed with a Soviet-made AKM assault rifle. Two Russian F-1 grenades hung on his belt.

Two more guards, dressed and armed more or less in the same manner as their comrade, were stationed at the ridge at the top of the valley. All three sentries seemed to pay more attention to the base below than any threat that might be closing in on them.

"Odds could be better," Lieutenant Reardon whispered to Yakov Katzenelenbogen. "Do you still want us to hold back while you and your mates move in first?"

Katz turned to the young Recce officer. The Recon Commando wore a brown fatigue uniform with a matching bush hat with a battered rim. Ammo belts for his R-4 rifle formed an X pattern across his chest and a large survival knife hung from his belt. Katz nodded firmly.

"First thing we have to do is try to rescue Lincoln and Finley," Katz said. "That's a bit tricky and there's no way we can be absolutely certain what we try will work."

"Pick off the guards and tell those Yanks to stay put while we handle the rough stuff," Reardon suggested.

"The only problem with that is the fact there's another bastard in the cave with Lincoln and Finley," McCarter explained as he fitted a bolt to the groove of his Barnett Commando crossbow. The Briton peered through the Bushnell scope mounted to the weapon.

"Yeah," Manning added. "And he'll kill them both if he gets the chance."

"We just have to make certain that doesn't happen," Calvin James remarked, carrying a large coil of nylon rope around his shoulder. "Well, cut down the chances of it happening, anyway."

"Timing is critical," Katz reminded his men. "Everything must go swiftly and smoothly. A lot of people are relying on us. Let's not disappoint them."

"Let's get in position and hit the bastards, damn it," David McCarter growled impatiently.

"I hate it when you say something that makes sense," Manning told the Briton. "Luckily, that doesn't happen very often."

The commando unit closed in slowly. The area was rugged, and had numerous boulders and rock formations for natural cover. The Recon Commandos were accustomed to using natural camouflage, and they were perfect soldiers for this sort of mission.

Katz, Sergeant Major Oktoba and two Recces surreptitiously approached one of the sentries stationed at the summit of the valley. The Israeli war-horse carried his most trusted weapon, the Uzi submachine gun. A foot-long sound suppressor was attached to the barrel. Oktoba and the two Recces were armed with R-4 rifles. Katz turned to the others and held an open palm at chest level to signal them to halt. He nodded at Oktoba. The BSS sergeant major laid down his R-4 and unbuckled his gunbelt.

Calvin James, David McCarter and a Recce sergeant moved in from the west. James was armed with his M-16 and Colt Commander. McCarter carried his two pet weapons, the Ingram M-10 and Browning Hi-Power pistol, as well as the Barnett crossbow. The Recce NCO hauled a 7.62 mm FN light machine gun with a bipod mount at the barrel. Ammo belts for the weapon crisscrossed the troopie's torso. James slithered to the cover of a stout, cone-shaped boulder. He patted the rock. It was perfect, James decided as he unslung the rope from his shoulder.

Gary Manning, Lieutenant Reardon and two other Recon Commandos approached from the north, moving toward the other sentry positioned at the rim of the valley. The

Canadian warrior carried his FAL rifle, equipped with a
Bushnell scope and a twelve-inch silencer. The .357 Eagle
pistol rode in leather under his arm, and the backpack of
plastic explosives was strapped to his back. Reardon and his
men carried R-4 rifles. One Recce also had a Heckler &
Koch 69A1 40 mm grenade launcher. Manning gestured for
the others to halt. The Canadian adopted a prone position,
aimed his FAL at the sentry and fixed his eye to the scope.

Karl Hahn and two Recon Commandos closed in from
the east. The German BND agent carried an H&K MP-5 and
his trusty Walther P-5 double-action automatic. The Recces
under his command were armed with R-4 rifles and two
American-made Claymore mines. Hahn signaled for his
team to halt. Their objective was the mine road extending
into the valley. The trio huddled behind a cluster of boulders and waited for the fireworks to start.

Captain Erik Hermann, the unit commander of the Recon Commandos participating in the raid, remained several hundred yards behind Katz's team. Hermann and the
remaining three Recce troopies were well armed with FN
light machine guns in addition to their assault rifles. Most
of the Recces carried side arms, either 9 mm NATO FN au-
tomatics or Beretta 92-SB double-action pistols. Each wore
a sturdy survival knife on his belt.

The strike force was in position, each section relying on
the other to reach its station and prepare for action. Each
man would depend on his teammates to act swiftly and ef-
ficiently when the battle began. This was the quality of the
fighting elite that formed a bond stronger than a blood re-
lationship.

Sergeant Major Oktoba was ready. He had stripped off
his uniform shirt and taken a small leather bag from a trou-
ser pocket. He grinned at Yakov Katzenelenbogen as he removed a plastic tube and squirted red ink across his white
undershirt. Oktoba's hand shook slightly. None of the

commandos blamed him for being nervous. Oktoba's role in the mission was critical and extremely dangerous.

Oktoba stepped from cover and staggered toward the sentry at the summit of the valley. He was totally unarmed. Oktoba clutched the leather bag in one hand and held his other hand to his crimson-stained chest. He stumbled forward, head bowed as he mumbled in Swahili. The guard gasped with surprise and swung his AKM rifle toward the sound of Oktoba's voice.

"Dhahabu," Oktoba groaned. *"Kamata dhahabu... saidia... tafadhali..."*

The sentry held his fire. This stranger appeared to be wounded. He was asking for help in Swahili, but this did not interest the Congolese gunman. However, Oktoba's moans of *dhahabu*—gold—immediately appealed to the sentry.

"Dhahabu... tafadhali...." Oktoba continued as he fell to his knees.

The BSS sergeant major dropped the leather pouch and clasped both hands to his chest. He fell on his back, still moaning and begging for help. The sentry barely noticed Oktoba's pleas. His attention was locked on the gold Krugerrand coins that spilled from the mouth of the sack.

The guard glanced across the valley at his fellow sentry. The other man stared at him, obviously wondering what might be wrong. The guard waved and shook his head to assure his comrade there was nothing to worry about. Why let the others know about the Krugerrands when he could have all the gold for himself?

The sentry approached Oktoba, stepping beyond the view of the other guard. A fistful of gold coins was too great a lure to ignore. He wondered if the wounded stranger had been shot stealing the Krugerrands from a white Afrikaner. If anyone was tracking the fugitive, they might find the secret base. The sentry decided he would have to report the stranger to his superiors. But no one needed to know about the gold.

As the sentry leaned over to grab the pouch, Katz triggered his Uzi. The silenced subgun sputtered harshly, and three 9 mm Parabellum rounds smashed into the sentry's chest. He fell to the ground, more astonished than pained by the bullets that drilled his heart and lungs. He opened his mouth, uttered a single choked groan and died.

"How'd I do?" Oktoba whispered as he sat up.

"You deserve an Academy Award," Katz replied, moving toward the sergeant major. "And a medal for bravery."

"Maybe I'll get to keep these," Oktoba said, grinning as he scooped up the bag of Krugerrands.

JAMES AND MCCARTER SAW the first sentry had been taken out. The Briton moved toward the rim of the valley ridge, his Barnett crossbow held ready. James and the Recce sergeant hastily wrapped one end of the rope around the cone-shaped boulder. They knotted the line securely. James gathered up the rest of the rope and headed for the cliff.

When the sentry on the north ridge saw the three commandos, his jaw fell open and his eyes widened with surprise. Then his face exploded when Gary Manning fired his FAL sniper rifle. A 7.62 mm projectile bit the base of his skull and burst a gory exit at the bridge of the guard's nose. The orbital bones cracked and the man's eyeballs popped from their sockets. The guard did not care. He was already dead.

McCarter aimed his crossbow at the Congolese killer stationed on the ledge near the cave that Phoenix Force suspected to be the cell block. The cross hairs of the scope found the side of the sentry's head, and the British warrior squeezed the trigger of the Barnett. The bowstring sung a single sharp note as the bolt sizzled from the crossbow. Sharp steel struck the guard's left temple, and the projectile split bone and pierced the man's brain. He collapsed on the ledge, the short fiberglass shaft jutting from his skull like a bizarre antler.

Calvin James tossed the rope over the cliff. The line fell into place, dangling at the mouth of the cave. James held the rope in his fists, braced his feet at the rock lip of the cliff and began to descend the rock wall.

James heard activity below, and he glanced up at McCarter. The Briton cocked the Barnett crossbow and took a new bolt from the scabbard on his left hip. A voice cried out from the enemy camp. Someone had seen James. He continued to descend the rock wall to the cave.

Several enemy troops stared up at the figure that moved toward the cave. To the terrorists, James resembled a giant spider dangling from a thick strand of webbing. Voices shouted warnings and alerted the rest of the camp. Two men raised their rifles. Then Manning's silenced FAL sniper weapon coughed, and the top of the gunman's head exploded. McCarter's crossbow sang, and a bolt slammed into the chest of the other rifleman, who was about to draw a bead on Calvin James.

The black commando reached the mouth of the cave, swung through the gap and released the rope. James landed inside the cave, knees bent to absorb the impact when his feet hit the stone floor. The Congolese gunman stationed by the cell aimed his Skorpion machine pistol at the iron bars. James fired his Colt Commander twice, and the gunman's body hopped and convulsed as the big .45-caliber slugs crashed into the killer. The guard fell against a wall of the cave and started to slump to the bottom. James shot him once more, pumping a 185-grain Silvertip round between the gunsel's eyes.

"Lord and Savior, Jesus Christ," Reverend Lincoln cried. He was on his knees, eyes tightly shut and fingers interlaced in prayer. "Grant me salvation! Please, God! Forgive me!"

James's ears were ringing painfully from the thunderous report of his .45 Colt within the confines of the cave, and he could barely hear what Lincoln said, but it was obvious the reverend was not talking to him, anyway. Senator Finley had flung himself in a corner and covered his head with his arms when the guard aimed the Skorpion at the prisoners. Neither man looked at James. Neither realized their would-be executioner now lay dead.

The American VIPs were still alive. That was all that concerned Calvin James at the moment. He just hoped neither man had a heart attack before he could get them out of there. Ironically, the pair were safe inside the cell, and James did not want two bumbling civilians to get in his way. He left them locked in the cell as he headed for the mouth of the cave.

The enemy camp was now fully aware of the raid. Figures scrambled from tents and trucks. Voices cried out in several languages. James holstered his Colt and unslung the M-16 assault rifle from his shoulder. He decided to ignore the human targets for the moment and turned his attention to the trucks parked in the terrorist stronghold.

James triggered the M-203 launcher attached to the barrel of his weapon. A 40 mm round of HE destruction plunged into one of the deuce-and-a-half vehicles. The truck exploded in a great fireball, and flaming gasoline splashed the canvas corner of the second vehicle. Two terrorists dashed from the burning wreckage, flames dancing along their backs and shoulders. Fire rampaged through their hair as they shrieked in agony. James hosed the pair with full-auto M-16 rounds to terminate their suffering forever.

The terrorists were disoriented. Caught off guard and subjected to sniper fire and explosions, most scurried about like panicked ants. Major Kingston and the ten mercenaries in his delegation were more experienced and better trained, and took cover among boulders along the rock walls.

"Work your way to the main tunnel," the merc commander ordered. "From there we can hold up with plenty of supplies and ammunition!"

Tai Skrubu's troops did not respond as well. Some ran for cover while others charged forward, firing their weapons at the rock walls although no clear targets were visible. Yakov Katzenelenbogen looked down at the Congolese gunmen and shook his head. Dealing with most of the terrorists would be like dynamiting a goldfish in a *koi* pool. Of course, there is nothing sporting about terrorism. One combats this human vermin with tactics as ruthless and uncompromising as those of the terrorist himself.

Phoenix Force and their South African allies moved in to the cliffs surrounding the enemy camp. The Recces set up the two FN light machine guns. Other troopies aimed their R-4 assault rifles. Others pulled the pins from grenades. Weapons erupted, spraying the terrorist base with a monsoon of high-velocity bullets. Volleys of 5.56 mm and 7.62 mm rounds chipped into a dozen Congolese troops.

Grenades were lobbed into the enemy camp. Tents burst apart. Mangled remains of terrorist bodies hurtled into the sky among the debris.

Three Congolese troops decided their best chance of survival was to launch a bold charge. The trio leaped into a jeep and bolted for the inclined road. Karl Hahn watched the vehicle roar up the gravel-covered slope. He pressed the charging button of an electrical squib as the jeep climbed halfway up the incline. A Claymore mine blasted a merciless wave of antipersonnel shrapnel. The explosion smashed the jeep like the steel-clad fist of a giant. The flaming remnants of the vehicle were scattered across the gravel. What remained of the three terrorists could have been buried in a shoe box.

A Congo-bred killer aimed a Soviet-made RP-6 rocket launcher at the raiders positioned along the cliffs above. He triggered the explosive projectile, and the rocket crashed into the lip of the ridge where Captain Hermann had set up a machine-gun team. The fierce explosion blasted loose half a ton of rock, and the bodies of two Recces sailed over the cliff and plunged two hundred feet to the base of the valley. The twisted metal remains of an FN machine gun and the butchered corpses of Hermann and another troopie were splattered across the ridge.

"Son of a bitch," Gary Manning rasped as he reached for the pack of explosives beside him. "I'm tired of being nice to these bastards."

He took a plastic disk from the pack. The object resembled a blue-and-white Frisbee, but it featured a circular timing mechanism at the center. Manning switched on the dial for five seconds, activated the detonator and hurled the disk at the position of the Congolese rocket man.

The flying saucer whirled into the enemy base. The terrorists were surprised as they watched the colorful missile gracefully float into their position. It did not seem to be a weapon, yet why had the invaders thrown it at them? The answer came when the Frisbee exploded. Five ounces of C-4 blasted the rocket man and three of his comrades. The explosion also ripped apart the cab of the only remaining deuce-and-a-half. The third and last truck blew apart, jetting flaming petrol and flying metal shards in all directions.

Major Kingston and his mercs broke cover and dashed for the shelter of the main tunnel. Four of his soldiers of fortune did not reach their objective. Bursts of 5.56 mm bullets from vengeful Recon Commandos cut the mercs down. Their bodies tumbled across the ground as the major and what remained of his troops scurried to the mouth of the tunnel.

"Mein Gott," Sergeant Gerber said with a breathless gasp. "What do we do now, Herr Major?"

"We defend this position," Kingston replied, glancing about at the cases of food, ammunition, weapons and explosives. "We've got enough here to fight a bloody war. We're protected on three sides by tons of rock and they'd have to blow up half this valley to cause a cave-in."

"Ja," the German merc remarked. "But I am not so sure they won't do exactly that, Herr Major."

21

Nyundo knelt beside Tai Skrubu. The Bantu warrior helplessly stared into the lifeless face of his master. Skrubu had been struck in the face and chest by flying shrapnel. Blood poured from a hundred cuts and gashes as Nyundo hopelessly tried to pull shards from Skrubu's flesh and stop the bleeding at the same time. Despite his great size and strength, the bodyguard could not save his master. Skrubu had died in Nyundo's arms.

Bitter tears of failure trickled down the tattooed cheeks of the Bantu fighting man. The battle was lost and his master was dead. All that remained for Nyundo was to die in a manner that would honor his Brothers of the Lion sect. The Bantu drew his Stechkin machine pistol, gathered up his war lance and crept from the boulders that had shielded him from bullets and explosions during the battle.

Virtually all the Congolese troops had been wiped out. Phoenix Force and the Recon Commandos were concentrating on Major Kingston's mercenaries at the main mine tunnel. The raiders and the mercs exchanged shots, neither able to get a clear target. No one noticed Nyundo charge up the incline. Black smoke from burning tires of jeeps and trucks helped conceal the Bantu as he jogged along the gravel path to the top of the summit.

Nyundo opened fire with his Stechkin the moment he saw Karl Hahn and the two Recces under the BND agent's command. Two bullets smashed into the frame of Hahn's

H&K chopper as he tried to point the weapon at the formidable Bantu. The impact ripped the MP-5 from the German commando's hands.

The two Recon troopies were not as fortunate. Both men were struck squarely in the chest by a volley of Russian Parabellums. The Recces collapsed. One man fell to his knees, wheezing violently as blood spewed from his mouth and nostrils. Nyundo fired another burst of Stechkin slugs into the wounded South African, shattering his skull like an eggshell.

The Bantu turned his weapon toward Hahn, his finger still pressed on the trigger. Smoke curled from the muzzle of the Stechkin, but no flame. Nyundo had used up the entire magazine. He tossed the machine pistol aside and lunged with his war lance.

"Leck mich am Arsch!" Karl Hahn snarled. "Kiss my ass!"

He pulled his Walther P-5 from shoulder leather and fired two 9 mm rounds into Nyundo's broad chest. The Bantu bellowed in rage and pain. He staggered and almost fell, bracing himself with the shaft of his lance. Nyundo glared at Hahn and charged once more.

Karl Hahn shot him in the face. A 115-grain flat-nosed bullet crashed through the bridge of Nyundo's nose. The Bantu fell forward, the point of his spear stabbing the ground. He slid along the length of the shaft until his forehead touched the earth. Hahn gripped his Walther with both hands to hold it steady as he aimed carefully and pumped a final bullet into the back of Nyundo's skull.

"GET US OUT OF HERE, DAMN IT!" Senator Finley snapped.

"Shut up," Calvin James replied gruffly as he tore a small chunk of CV-38 from a wad of plastic explosives. "I don't want to make any mistakes with this stuff, man. Unless you want to take a chance on having the roof of your cell fall down on your head, just be quiet so I can concentrate.''

The senator and Reverend Lincoln clamped their mouths shut. James wished Gary Manning was with him. The Canadian demolitions expert had instructed James in the use of CV-38, but the black warrior was unfamiliar with the British low-velocity explosive. The lock to the cell did not look very impressive, but James did not intend to break his foot trying to kick down an iron door.

''Why don't you shoot the lock?'' Lincoln asked.

''You've seen too many movies,'' James muttered, fitting the chunk of plastic explosive into the lock. ''If a bullet ricochets off this thing it'll be chasin' us around in this cave. Now, move away from the bars and turn your faces toward the wall. Cover your ears and open your mouths. Don't turn around until I tell you to.''

The captives obeyed instructions. James inserted a pencil detonator and switched it for ten seconds. He did not care much for explosives and wanted to get as far away from the blast as circumstances allowed.

The CV-38 spoke not with a bang, but a sputtering pop. The iron door creaked open, smoke drifting from the blasted lock. James told Finley and Lincoln to haul ass. All three men moved to the mouth of the cave where a leather harness, similar to a parachute rig, hung from the rope. McCarter and the Recce sergeant had not gone to sleep. They had pulled up the line and secured the harness before returning the rope to its position.

Lincoln and Finley hesitated. The commandos were still trading shots with the mercs at the tunnel, but none of the Congolese troops were left and no one was shooting at the west wall. James abruptly shoved the senator into the harness. Finley objected as James tried to fasten the buckle. The black warrior sighed and sharply backhanded the senator across the face.

"We don't have time for this shit," James barked. "Some good men have been killed in this rescue mission. I'm not so sure either one of you dudes is worth the sacrifices made to get you outta here. So don't fuck with me or you'll both go back to the States with your jaws wired together."

Neither man protested again. McCarter and the Recon NCO pulled the rope and hauled Finley up to the ridge. When the senator was free of the harness, they lowered it for Lincoln. After the reverend was safe, the harness returned for Calvin James.

David McCarter grinned as he slapped James on the back.

"Bloody show-off," the Briton said. "But you did a good job anyway, mate."

"Thanks," James replied, "but what are we going to do about those assholes in the mine?"

"Hell," McCarter said with a shrug. "They're not going anywhere."

He unclipped a walkie-talkie from his belt and pressed the Transmit button. "Wallburg, this is Nelson," McCarter said into the mouthpiece. "Do you read me? Over."

"Read you, Nelson," the voice of Yakov Katzenelenbogen replied. "Are Finley and Lincoln safe? Over."

"That's what I called to tell you," McCarter said. "They're right here with us. Safe and sound. Over."

"Good," Katz announced. "Get them out of there. We're pulling out immediately. Over."

"Pulling out?" The Briton frowned. "What about those blokes in the tunnel?"

"Forget about them," Katz told him. "I received a message from Aerial Recon. A plane was picked up on radar. It's heading in our direction and it does not have clearance to be here. Attempts to contact the pilot by radio have been ignored. It was sighted by the Recces at the gunship waiting to pick us up. They think it's carrying some sort of barrels on its underbelly."

"Jesus," Calvin James whispered.

"Pull out," Katz insisted. "Over and out."

The Phoenix Force assault unit and the two liberated Americans hurried from the area as a dot appeared in the sky. The commandos pulled and shoved Finley and Lincoln as they broke into a double-time march. A bumblebee hum announced the approach of a single-engine Beech. The hum slowly grew louder.

"Hit the dirt!" Katz ordered.

The commandos followed instructions and pulled the two civilian VIPs down with them. Less than a quarter of a mile away and about seven hundred feet from the ground, the Beech aircraft flew toward the McClearry copper mine.

Stoyan Kostadinov had been flying around the Orange Free State for over an hour and a half, trying to home in on the faint beeping signal on the radio receiver the KGB had installed in his plane. The beep was much stronger now, and the valley below appeared to be the target.

His hands were wet with sweat as he cruised over the abandoned mine site. Kostadinov was afraid to make a pass and check the area below. He did not want to see anyone in the valley before he dropped the drums on them. He was also afraid someone might shoot him down if he seemed suspicious. The Bulgarian mole prayed to a God he was not supposed to believe in as he triggered the release button.

Major Kingston and two of his mercs had ventured from the tunnel. The mercenary commander smiled when he saw the cliffs were no longer crawling with commandos. He frowned when he heard the engine of a plane and glanced up to see the underside of Kostadinov's Beech. Kingston screamed in sheer terror when he saw the drums fall from the aircraft.

The barrels plunged to the base of the valley, and Kostadinov elevated his Beech and sped away as the drums exploded. The valley resembled a volcano as burning liquid spewed up from the mining complex. A violent tremor rippled through the earth beneath the men of Phoenix Force and their allies. Flames leaped from the valley as if hell had burst up from the ground.

"Holy shit!" Gary Manning said, gasping as he stared at the chemical blaze that consumed the McClearry mine. "That was the biggest Molotov cocktail I've ever seen."

"Anybody get the number of that hit-and-run flyer?" James inquired.

"There's no hurry to identify the pilot or his aircraft," Karl Hahn commented. "They'll catch him eventually. Sort of a pity. The fellow did us a favor without realizing it."

"What the hell was that?" Finley inquired in a stunned voice.

"Unless I'm guessing up the wrong theory," Katz replied, taking a walkie-talkie from his belt, "that was somebody doing a little job for the Soviets. We'll explain later. Right now, I'm going to contact our gunship pilot so we can get a ride back to civilization."

"Lord be praised," Reverend Lincoln said with a sigh of relief. "It's finally over."

"Amen," Calvin James agreed with a weary nod.

Mack Bolan's

PHOENIX FORCE

by Gar Wilson

Schooled in guerrilla warfare, equipped with all the
latest lethal hardware, Phoenix Force battles the powers
of darkness in an endless crusade for freedom, justice
and the rights of the individual. Follow the adventures
of one of the legends of the genre. Phoenix Force is the
free world's foreign legion!

"Gar Wilson is excellent! Raw action attacks the reader
on every page."

—Don Pendleton

GOLD EAGLE

Phoenix Force titles are available
wherever paperbacks are sold.

Mack Bolan's

ABLE TEAM

by Dick Stivers

Action writhes in the reader's own street as Able Team's Carl "Mr. Ironman" Lyons, Pol Blancanales and Gadgets Schwarz make triple trouble in blazing war. To these superspecialists, justice is as sharp as a knife. Join the guys who began it all—Dick Stivers's Able Team!

"This guy has a fertile mind and a great eye for detail. Dick Stivers is brilliant!"

—Don Pendleton

Able Team titles are available wherever paperbacks are sold.

GOLD EAGLE

TAKE 'EM NOW

FOLDING SUNGLASSES FROM GOLD EAGLE

Mean up your act with these tough, street-smart shades. Practical, too, because they fold 3 times into a handy, zip-up polyurethane pouch that fits neatly into your pocket. Rugged metal frame. Scratch-resistant acrylic lenses. Best of all, they can be yours for only $6.99. **MAIL ORDER TODAY.**

Send your name, address, and zip code, along with a check or money order for just $6.99 + .75¢ for postage and handling (for a total of $7.74) payable to Gold Eagle Reader Service, a division of Worldwide Library. New York and Arizona residents please add applicable sales tax.

Remove from pouch...

unfold once...

GOLD EAGLE
In USA:
901 Fuhrmann Blvd.
P.O. Box 1394
Buffalo, N.Y. 14240-9963

unfold twice...

and they're ready to wear.

GES1-R